A ROAD OF STARS

BORGO PRESS BOOKS BY ARDATH MAYHAR

The Absolutely Perfect Horse (with Marylois Dunn)
Carrots and Miggle
Crazy Quilt: The Best Short Stories of Ardath Mayhar
Deadly Memoir: A Novel of Suspense
The Door in the Hill: A Tale of the Turnipins
The Dropouts: A Tale of Growing Up in East Texas
Feud at Sweetwater Creek: A Novel of the Old West
The Fugitives: A Tale of Prehistoric Times
The Heirs of Three Oaks: A Novel of the Old West
How the Gods Wove in Kyrannon: Tales of the Triple Moons
Hunters of the Plains: A Novel of Prehistoric America
Island in the Lake: A Novel of Native America
Khi to Freedom: A Science Fiction Novel
The Lintons of Skillet Bend
Lone Runner: A Novel of the Old West
Lords of the Triple Moons: Tales of the Triple Moons
Makra Choria: A Novel of High Fantasy
Medicine Dream: The Further Adventures of Burr Henderson
Messengers in White: A Science Fantasy Novel
Monkey Station (Macaque Cycle #1; with Ron Fortier)
People of the Mesa: A Novel of Native America
A Planet Called Heaven: A Science Fiction Novel
Prescription for Danger: A Novel of the Old West
Reflections; &, Journey to an Ending: Collected Poems
A Road of Stars: A Fantasy of Life, Death, Love, and Art
Runes of the Lyre: A Science Fantasy Novel
The Saga of Grittel Sundotha: A Science Fantasy Novel
The Seekers of Shar-Nuhn: Tales of the Triple Moons
*Slewfoot Sally and the Flying Mule: Tall Tales from Cotton
    County, Texas*
Soul-Singer of Tyrnos: A Fantasy Novel
Strange Doings in the Pine Hills: Stories of Fantasy and Mystery
Through a Stone Wall: Lessons from Thirty Years of Writing
Timber Pirates: A Novel of East Texas (with Marylois Dunn)
Towers of the Earth: A Novel of Native America
*Trail of the Seahawks (*Macaque Cycle #2; with Ron Fortier)
Warlock's Gift: Tales of the Triple Moons
The World Ends in Hickory Hollow
A World of Weirdities: Tales to Shiver By

A ROAD OF STARS

A Fantasy of Life, Death, Love, and Art

by

Ardath Mayhar

The Borgo Press
An Imprint of Wildside Press LLC

MMVIII

CONTENTS

FOREWORD

A need to dance—not social dancing but ballet—has run in my family since the time of my great-grandmother Ellington, who would "get the spirit" and dance all over the Methodist Church, which abhorred the very notion of dance in the late Nineteenth Century. My aunt also had the impulse, but had no access to training until she was too old to benefit from it. I danced as soon as I could walk, but again, the right sort of training was unavailable in my small East Texas town when I was a child. I think and believe that Cornelia Watson's total dedication to her art is the sort that I, at least, might well have devoted to dancing, if I had had the chance.

—Ardath Mayhar
Chireno, Texas
July 2007

A Road of Stars, by Ardath Mayhar

A ROAD OF STARS, BY ARDATH MAYHAR

Lie quietly:
delineate the intricate maze,
the bright-hot paths of pain;
see the light-traced map
drawn inwardly,
stabbed with stars of anguish
where mortality passes.

Lie quietly:
upon insides of eyelids
project astronomers' charts
of systems and galaxies;
envision magnetic fields
gemmed with suns'
interlocking orbits.

Lie quietly:
overlay the shining patterns
in a starry web of pain.

A Road of Stars, by Ardath Mayhar

CHAPTER ONE

THE HARD WAY

The dying woman opened her eyes.

Skewered upon her penetrating gray gaze, the speaker paused in mid-syllable, his mouth opening and closing silently. He coughed to cover his confusion, trying to find his momentum again, but it was no use. He sputtered to a stop.

"Absolutely not," said Cornelia Watson. Her voice was quiet, gruff with the fluid that plagued her, as well as with pain.

"We can prolong your life by months!" the doctor said. "New medications and techniques are being developed every day. It's insane to turn your back on the chance of living!"

"Living?" Her voice held passion and pain. "Do you call this living? Look at those photographs on the wall, and then turn and look at me. Think what it will be like for me, from now until I die. Look me squarely in the eyes and tell me that I am condemned to live!"

The gray eyes closed as the doctor turned to the wall of photos. All were of the same woman, Cornelia Watson as the Dying Swan, as Odette and Odile in Swan Lake, as the Firebird and dozens of other major roles from the classic repertory, as well as action shots from her own works.

She could see, inside her eyelids, what he saw. She had lived those roles a thousand times. She knew the feeling of the music along her bones, as she made motion of the choreographer's dream. She knew the rush of excitement when a piece of music entered her own mind and body and shaped itself into a dance that only she could envision and express.

11

She opened her eyes, seeing the round face now turned toward her. His expression, his plump, worried face told her what he was seeing, even though she could watch her own deterioration in the huge mirror on the wall facing her bed. The grossly swollen bulk that had been that lissome body always stared back.

Her niece thought it was sick, having that mirror there. "It's masochism," Lisa had told her. "Pure masochism!"

But Cornelia knew it was only Truth, and she had never been afraid of that. It had been the thing that motivated her muscles and bones as she worked. Truth kept her entire being focused upon her goals, no matter how painful or lonely or complicated her personal life became. If the truth of what she was happened to be that dropsical woman reflected in the glass, then so be it.

She would neither deny nor ignore it.

The doctor's voice overrode her thoughts. "You're still a young woman! Forty-three is barely into middle age, nowadays. Your life is valuable to a lot of people, even if you can't dance any longer. There are other things than dance."

"For other people perhaps." Her face flamed with anger. "I am a dancer. I have had no other life, even though I always understood that the body would go, at last. I could have taught or continued to choreograph, or both. I could live with that, but now I can't even move without agony.

"I cannot exist without motion. If it brings breathlessness and pain, then I will not persist in clinging to life."

She stared at the doctor. "Dr. Howard, why is it that you are so afraid of dying?"

His round face turned pink with shock. "I see death every day," he protested. "I have no fear of it."

"Not of death. Of dying, yourself, personally. And if you fear it, why is that so?"

He didn't answer. Instead, he polished his bifocals carefully and replaced them on his nose. "You are hysterical. I shall return tomorrow, and we will decide which hospital you prefer."

She gave a great effort and pulled herself up on the pillows. Her heart thudded soggily with the stress, but she ignored it. "I will not be here. I will not see you again. I am going home."

"I cannot agree to that. It could be fatal."

"I am sane, free, and I choose to go home."

He turned even pinker. He waved his hands and his carefully modulated voice grew shrill with protest. She was quite exhausted when he ran down at last, but her intention was unchanged. At last he understood that, without her saying another word. He turned, took his bag, and left the room.

Cornelia lay back against her pillows, which were piled against the head of her bed. To be able just to lie flat without the threat of suffocation seemed to her a blessing that she had never appreciated. Her puffy hand moved to touch the small bell on the table, and its musical note brought Amanda into the room.

"He tired you out, didn't he?" the older woman asked. She moved to straighten the coverlet, plump the pillows, remove all trace of the doctor's presence from the room.

"Told you you were crazy to think of staying out of the hands of the medical people, didn't he? I knew he'd do that. They just can't stand the thought of anybody dying naturally and in their own time."

Cornelia laughed. She was too weary, and it joggled her fluid-filled tissues too much for comfort, but she couldn't help it. In her present condition, if she had some soft-footed, gentle-voiced companion who insisted on soothing her reverently, it would have driven her mad. Amanda, on the contrary, was as bracing as a gust of sleet in the face.

"He had kittens when I said I was going home. He would really have a litter if I had told him where home is." She chuckled, lying back, every muscle limp with exhaustion.

For much of the afternoon she slept. When Amanda brought her tea and milk toast, she woke to find the windows pink with sunset light.

"Call Lucius," she said, stirring her tea with a spoon that had belonged to her grandmother. She felt the holly pattern under the ball of her thumb, and its familiar lines brought her mother sharply into her memory. She had handled any problem she faced with style and decisiveness. Her daughter would do no less.

"You finally going to make your will?" asked Amanda. She was sitting beside the desk, holding her teacup on her knee and thumbing through a magazine. "About time, if you hold to your schedule."

Cornelia nodded. "I wanted to think out just what I want to do before putting it all onto paper. In the morning, will you call Miss Carling and ask her to visit me? I want the paintings back, for a while.

"Assure her that I am not recalling the loan permanently. I just want them while I can enjoy them.

"When I die, most will go to the museum permanently. That is one thing that is going into the will. I do need to study those lovely pieces again...there has never been time, before now." She set her empty cup on the bedside table and leaned back more deeply into the pillows. Her breath came very short, nowadays.

"*The Road to Sainte Angele*," she breathed. "*Lane Among Pine Trees*." She sighed, visualizing the paintings that she had bought all over the world as she toured with her company. Every one depicted a road or a lane, a path or a track or a street, each in its own unique setting in some distant part of the world that she had passed through in a whirl of performances, without being able to afford the time to explore it.

"No sweat," said Amanda. "Want me to call Amos to get the house ready?"

"Yes. Have the electricity reconnected, the propane tank filled, and a phone put in. Eric should be able to help him get that done, and things should be ready by the time I finish my business here and make the trip."

"You're going to fly, the shape you're in?"

Cornelia grinned wickedly at her old friend. "You know me too well, Amanda. I am going to do just that, and if Howard will not give me the go-ahead, I know doctors who will. If I die on the way, what the hell? Everything will go to Lisa in good order, except for the bequests."

She would have thought Amanda's grin as wicked as her own, if she hadn't noticed the moisture in the corners of the old woman's eyes. She had been Cornelia's family ever since the days when she had been one of the wardrobe mistresses with the company. When her arthritis became too painful to allow her to sew, Cornelia had hired her as maid and companion, and now she shuddered to think what her present life would be without her.

"I hope you invested your money wisely," she said suddenly.

Amanda looked up. "Got Lucius to handle it for me. He says it'll keep me in style for as long as I'm likely to last. It was good sense for you to give it to me ahead of time, he told me; that way there's no chance of your heirs questioning it, and you know Lisa would.

"Besides, as long as I'm working, it just sits there and draws interest. I'll probably have a little nest-egg to leave my grandson."

Cornelia tried to draw a deep breath, but her fluid-soaked lungs defeated her. She sank deeply into the pillows, tired. So tired. And there was still so much to be done!

* * * * * * *

Lucius arrived promptly at ten o'clock the next morning. He knew her schedule, as well as the depth of her weariness, which grew worse day by day. He sat beside her bed and took notes, as she enumerated her assets and listed the bequests and the disposition of the bulk of the estate.

"Put it into trust for ten years," she told him. "I have worked out a schedule to give her what she needs along the way but which will not allow her to go overboard or to be a temptation to bloodsuckers." Cornelia knew too well the sort of slug who battened upon well-heeled women.

"I also want it written into the will, as well as into a directive to be given to my kin and my doctor, whoever that may be after I move, that I am not to be kept alive by artificial means. I want a certified copy to take with me.

"When you hear from Amanda that I am *in extremis*, I would like for you to come at once, if that seems necessary, to make sure that the doctors don't get their hooks into me."

"You know, my dear, that you have a fixation about that. Doctors do a lot of good. Many people are walking the streets who would be in their graves, without medical services." Lucius looked concerned.

"True. But I was there while my mother died by inches. I saw how they think and how they work. She would have died months earlier, if they had not treated her for pneumonia. I asked them to let her go, and they looked at me as if I'd proposed murder." She glared at the lawyer.

"They sentenced her to months of agony—they're the ones with fixations. The one thing we are all entitled to do is die. By heaven, I intend to go about my own death in my own way."

Before Lucius could reply, there came a rap at the door, which burst open to admit Lisa. Cornelia regarded her niece calmly, though Lisa was flushed and obviously upset.

"Are you mad?" the girl asked. "I just had a call from Dr. Howard, who is very concerned about you. He thinks you need psychiatric help. He said that I need to take over your affairs and force you to care for yourself."

"He thinks he can grind a few thousand dollars more out of me before I croak," said Cornelia. "Sit down, Lisa. Pull yourself together. You have met Lucius, I think?"

The girl glared at the lawyer, who smiled at her without rancor. Then Lisa leaned forward. "The legal beagle? What are you doing here?"

"If you cannot be civil, then go," said her aunt. "He is here attending to my business, as he often is. If you had been anywhere in my vicinity for the past many years, you would not ask such a stupid question.

"He has just made my will, and he is about to agree to help me to remove myself and certain of my possessions to my homeplace. To which you are welcome, as a guest on a non-permanent basis."

Lisa started up from her chair. "You are not telling me that you intend to go back to the farm? You have gone mad! Well, I can do something about that. There are such things as competency hearings!"

Lucius rose and took his briefcase from beneath his chair. "It would be a pity," he said. "We should be forced to

16

sue you for slander. And you would probably be left out of your aunt's will, if you took such an unwarranted and interfering step."

Lisa went red. Before she could speak, Lucius went on, "Dr. Leonard Harshaw is a close friend of Cornelia's. He was here Sunday for tea and a long talk, along with several other prominent people who recall your aunt's art fondly and her person even more so. I suspect that the word of the psychiatrist who literally 'wrote the book' would carry a lot of weight in such a case."

He bent to kiss Cornelia lightly on the forehead. "Goodbye, my dear. I'll bring this back tomorrow for signing. And I just may talk to Leonard, to make certain he will be available, if we need him."

He nodded to Lisa, but she only glared as the door closed behind his neatly tailored back.

"Aunt, I cannot understand you."

Cornelia smiled. "Not one of my family, except your father, ever could or did or wanted to. Thirty years ago, in rural East Texas, nice girls were not encouraged to study dancing. Nice girls did not turn down offers of marriage from eligible bachelors. Nice girls did not go to New York alone with fifteen dollars in their pockets. Nice girls, if they did such things, became Bad Girls. They did not succeed, as I did."

The girl pulled the small sewing rocker over to the bedside. "You know the family doesn't feel that way! They all admire you...you're the only Watson ever to be an international Name."

"When I began bringing in large sums for my efforts, they quieted a bit, although Aunt Emily still thinks I am a high-class call girl. Before that I was not welcome to visit anyone except your father.

"I got letters of the most unspeakable kind from your Aunt Coral and my Aunt Emily. They were, and still are, mortified to have a dancer in the family. They wanted me to change my name, so they wouldn't be disgraced by my activities. Surely you have heard about that."

Amanda came into the room with a determined air. "Time for your medicine," she said. "If you want to hold up

17

for the move home." She offered the paper cup and the water, and Cornelia swallowed obediently.

"Home!" Lisa bristled. "Why you want to go back to East Texas I'll never know. Back to the boondocks with nothing but armadillos and possums and rednecks. I wouldn't go back there if you paid me!"

"Wouldn't you?" Cornelia's tone was thoughtful. "I think you'd go anyplace, if the money was right. Unlike my brother Eric. But I do, indeed, intend to go home. You need not visit me there. I intend to suit myself, in this.

"I'll die where I want to die, when the good Lord sees fit. Now go tell Amanda that I think I can eat my lunch. Arguments make me hungry."

CHAPTER TWO

FORBIDDEN JOURNEY

Two weeks crept past. She examined and signed reams of papers and fidgeted while Amanda supervised the crating of her possessions. The older woman strawbossed the operation with relish, and Cornelia knew that things were done correctly, if at all. Lucius was in and out almost every day.

Cornelia knew that he hated to see her go. They had been friends for the better part of two decades. She had tried to help him deal with his wife's death, and he, in turn, had comforted her when she decided, after entirely too much hesitation, to send David on his way.

That had been a situation in which the intelligent decision that Lucius had been urging had not penetrated her mind as quickly as it should.

Thinking of David sent her into a fit of depression that lasted until the packing was completed and she had been moved into a hotel for the last two days in New York. No one liked behaving like a fool, particularly one like Cornelia, who had spent her life controlling her mind and body to the exclusion of everything else.

David had struck her carefully orchestrated existence with the impact of a meteor—or a bomb. The painstaking wall she had raised about her emotions crumbled, letting him into the narrow field of her feelings.

It had taken her five years to see through his facade of culture and intelligence, into the falseness of his pretended regard for her and her art.

Lucius warned her. She shut him out of her life for a time because of that, but he had tried his best to make her see. Amanda had scolded her, but she didn't listen.

"No fool like an old fool," Cornelia murmured, ignoring the fact that at the time she had been only a bit over thirty. Yet even that should have been too mature to allow a childish dream of romantic adventure to distract her from the dedication that was her life.

Only when she realized that she was neglecting her work had she sat down and looked at herself and David with the cold eye of reason. She had seen herself clearly, and she did not like what was revealed.

Her confrontation with David had been the most painful thing she had ever done in her less-than-painless existence. "I can't see you again," she told him.

She still remembered what she was wearing that night. They had gone to a reception after the performance, and she wore her black Givenchy with the long silver chain holding a single baguette diamond. She recalled gripping the pendant until it cut into her hand, as she spoke to the man she had thought she loved.

"I am not one who can choose emotional fulfillment over the work that I must do. Our companionship is becoming a distraction.

"I know now that what I need most is dance, not love's young dream." Her tone had been bitter, and the taste of the words still lingered on her tongue.

She had been too kind to say that she knew, at last, that the loans she made him would never be repaid. She regretted her forbearance, later, when her charge accounts showed large expenditures that she had not approved or allowed.

David looked stunned. His cool green eyes widened, and he had gone even paler than his usual bloodless hue. Even his white-blond hair had seemed to wilt, and then a flush rose under his thin British skin. The green eyes went dark with anger.

"I suppose you think that I will be devastated," he said. "But I intend to surprise you. You had the key to a world that I wanted to enter. Now I have contrived my own place there.

"You have money, and that was convenient, for a time, but now I have the means to make more of my own. You are decorative, and I may miss the stares that follow us through restaurants and theaters, but one cannot have everything."

She smiled grimly, now, glad that there had been another thing that he had not possessed. She had seen, over her years in her field, what intense love affairs did to her peers.

Sex was a terrible waste of energy, she had decided when very young. She had not been willing to invest that much of her life force in a purely emotional binge, and he had not been able to persuade her to. She did not have that to regret.

Lying in her hotel room, hearing for the last time the cacophony of traffic below her window, the distant sirens, the babble of life, she laughed, at last. Who, among all the people she had known, the big names and the hangers-on, the users and the helpers, would believe that Cornelia Watson, *ballerina extraordinaire*, toast of the Continent and New York, *grande dame* of dance, was going to her grave a virgin?

Amanda interrupted her thoughts. "We leave in the morning at ten. Horace will be here with the cab at nine forty-five, and we will have a moment to say goodbye to him. I'm going to miss that old villain more than any of the bigwigs in the Company.

"He'll get us to the airport by 10:30 at the latest, and our flight leaves at 11:05. I have arranged for a wheelchair to be waiting for you at Kennedy and again in Dallas. There isn't any use having to worry with your folding chair while we're en route."

"That sounds fine. Have you heard anything from Lisa?" Cornelia wasn't sure if she wanted to know.

"Not one word. I expected to get a call at any time, but there's been nothing. I did hear from Dr. Howard. He's still fuming about your decision to go home, but he didn't mention anything about having you declared incompetent. He'd better not—I'll incompetent him!"

"I will be glad to see Horace. That has been one of the really bad things about being helpless—my real friends, the doorman, Horace, the newslady on the corner—never get near enough for me to see them. At least, I will have the chance to tell Horace how much he has meant to me. A friend who drives a cab is to be priced above rubies!"

"What about Dmitri and the Arkady brothers? Are you going to call them this evening to say goodbye?" Amanda's tone was wry.

Cornelia's reply was obscene, pithy, and all too accurate. Amanda dropped into a chair, shaking with laughter.

"I couldn't agree more! Oh, and Miss Carlin has had the paintings packed and shipped. They should be waiting when we get there. I never really understood what goes on with you and those pictures. Just a lot of roads and paths, streets and tracks—I never heard of such a collection of art." Amanda looked puzzled, as she always did when she thought of Cornelia's paintings.

Cornelia smiled. All the roads she had never had time to explore were there in those paintings. All the things she had possessed neither time nor energy to do, to see, or to learn were there.

Now, if nothing more, she would have the time to allow her mind to wander those roads, seeing what might be beyond the bend in the forest trail, the rise of the desert highway, or the dip in the swampy path.

"I'm ready to go," she said. "Already I can hear the frogs croaking in the pond in the meadow, the crickets around the house in the four-o'clocks. Amanda, I'm going to live to get home. I don't know how much longer, but don't worry about my dying on you along the way."

But by the time she was ready to get on the plane she wasn't so sure. She hadn't counted on the emotional drain of saying goodbye to Horace.

Seated and strapped in at last, she wiped her eyes. Horace had driven her about the city for fifteen years. He almost always managed to be available when she needed him. Never had she been late; never had she waited more than a few minutes for his arrival.

Now she had seen his bearded face, his piratical moustache, and his kind black eyes for the last time. She didn't mind dying, she found, but she was learning that she hated goodbyes passionately.

The engines increased their noise to a roar that shook all the excess fluid in her body. She felt sick, but she held on, and once they got into the air she felt better.

Amanda, beside her, checked constantly, touching her wrist, looking into her face. For some reason, the old woman's concern didn't irritate her as that of others seemed to do.

She decided that she could sleep the hours of the flight away, perhaps easing the weariness that made her feel dizzy. She accepted a pillow and closed her eyes...

David waited behind her eyelids. Why? She was rid of him, permanently she was certain. He had felt nothing for her, and time had taught her that what she felt for him was nothing but flattered ego and frustrated emotion. But just before she dropped into sleep, Lisa, too, popped into her mind.

Why David and Lisa together? Something about the conjunction made her shiver, but she was, by then, asleep.

Dallas was a chaos of noise and people and hurry. The chair waited, and Amanda pushed her along, muttering impatiently as people grudgingly made way.

As they emerged into the main terminal, Cornelia exclaimed, "Look! There's Eric!"

Her brother took over with the ease of long experience. Her luggage was collected, the chair relinquished, and she was quickly installed in his travel van, which sat just outside the terminal in a spot reserved for VIPs and shuttle buses. Just like Eric!

She hadn't seen him in how long? Since his trip to Rome, five years ago. He looked older. Worried.

She found herself grinning widely as he checked the seatbelt and turned to give Amanda a hand into the rear of the van beside her.

"You never did give much of a damn what the family thought, did you, Eric?" she asked, once her heart settled into something like a normal rhythm. "Even when I was considered the Fallen Woman of the Watson clan, you stood by me. I should have known you would meet us here. Amanda called you, didn't she?"

"I would have scragged her if she hadn't," he said. She could see his square hands on the wheel. He had just had a haircut, and the back of his neck was paler just below the hairline than the checkered leather of his exposed skin.

"Your neck looks just like Papa's," she said. "Come to think of it, you sit just like Papa used to, sort of hunched over the wheel.

"Oh, Eric, it is so good to see you! I saw quite a bit of Lisa, before we left, but I don't know any of her plans. I intend to leave her what I have—you have more than enough, and I'll be damned if I leave anything to Coral and Aunt Emily."

"Coral's our sister." His tone was uncomfortable. "Don't forget that. She may be close-minded, but she is our parents' child."

Cornelia sighed with frustration. "I will never forgive the way she and Aunt Emily treated me when I first went away. If she says anything to you about visiting the poor dying invalid, you discourage her, you hear?"

Amanda turned to look at her. "You need to rest. Go to sleep, Cornelia. You want some help?"

Cornelia felt the fluid sloshing in her body. "No. I'll calm down, but I think I'm too keyed up to sleep." She leaned her head against the high back of the seat and closed her eyes.

When she opened them again, an hour later, the van was pulling up at a gas station just past Athens. The trees were the familiar ones of home, ash, elm, sweet gum, hickory, and pine...the first pines you saw, traveling south and east from Dallas.

The old man who ambled out to fill their tank looked a thousand years old and was probably forty. He grunted at Eric, who grunted back, and communication was established. She breathed as deeply as she could. The smell in the air was that of home. Even tanged with hot asphalt and gasoline fumes, it held the mellow scent of leaves and clover and fresh-cut grass.

She had lain awake in the city, the first months of her professional life, longing for a breath of that air. No matter where her performances took her, she had never lost her roots in the East Texas soil.

They arrived at Eric's house just after dark. Eric had a modest frame home well outside the city limit, and his neighbors lived at some distance. She looked around, as they lifted her into the folding wheelchair, at the night. The stars stared down from a midnight-black sky.

"I'm almost home!" she said.

Eric patted her shoulder and hurried ahead to open the door. Cynthia waited inside in the air-conditioned house, ignoring the scented wonder of the warm night.

Just like her sister-in-law, Cornelia thought. "I am so glad to see you again," she said aloud, knowing it for a lie.

Cynthia had never approved of her husband's loyalty to his errant sister. She and Coral were thick as thieves when they were girls, and things had never changed much.

Cynthia smiled stiffly. "My dear! I am just happy we can help." The effort behind her words was perfectly plain.

Eric might look stolid and tough, but he had a perceptiveness that nobody but his sister knew. He separated the two, wheeling Cornelia into her room, and sent his wife to the kitchen after sandwiches and coffee.

Once they were alone, he kissed her on the cheek. His eyes were filled with tears, and he dabbed at them with the back of his hand, unashamed.

"Hon, I hate to see you like this! You just don't know how it hurts. You were so lovely...you moved like a deer in the woods. It must be pure hell for you, now."

"God, Eric, it's so good to have somebody understand that! People pussyfoot around, trying to pretend that I don't look like some gross, awful slug, and I know exactly what I look like.

"How Amanda has stood it I don't know. And I won't bother you for long—just until I can get out to the house. Amos should come for me tomorrow with the station wagon."

Eric opened the door and took the tray from Cynthia's hands. "We'll just sit here and have a quiet talk," he told his wife. "I know you want to go to the bridge club meeting, and you might as well go ahead, Cyn. We have a lot of catching up to do."

"I am sure you do." Her tone was something between a purr and a snarl. "If there's anything you need, Eric can show you where to find it. Your woman can manage, I am sure."

"So I get tarred with the same brush," Amanda muttered, joining them as they listened to the departing car. "I'm Cornelia's friend, so I'm her enemy. Plain as day. No offense," she said, turning to Eric.

"I know my girl," he said. "Strange as it seems, she suits me fine, most of the time. And when she doesn't, I take off for Paris or Rome or San Francisco and tend to business until I get lonesome for her again. That's the best thing about being an importer...you always have a good excuse to travel."

Cornelia chuckled. "We're two of a kind, you know. Never did do anything by other people's rules. Never paid attention to what others might think. I'll bet you dollars to doughnuts that she thinks she rules you with an iron hand."

Eric leaned back and laughed. Then he rose and touched her shoulder lightly. "Sure enough! Now you get settled in and rest. Amanda, your room is right on the other side of the bath. You two sleep well, and if you need anything, just call me."

When the door closed behind him, Cornelia took a deep breath that sounded like a groan. Amanda, understanding at once, got her into bed and gave her the pain medication.

She fell headlong into sleep, and she did not dream at all.

CHAPTER THREE

BACKWARD JOURNEY

She knew that she was dreaming. This had happened many times, when she was a child; something she longed to do would become real as she slept. It would seem completely true, and yet some part of her always knew that it was only a dream and would end when she woke again.

. It was in that way she came to realize that she must dance. In her dreams she could leap high into the air, revolving as slowly as a bit of fluff riding an air current, to descend at her leisure.

She could, in the dream state, attain total control and complete absorption. It soon became necessary that she learn to do that in her waking life, as well.

By the time she was twelve, her teachers at Marisa's School of the Ballet Arts admitted that she had gone beyond them. Her mother, managing desperately to get the money for her lessons, had almost despaired. Aunt Emily had chortled, for she had fought bitterly to keep 'any niece of hers' from becoming a dancer.

But Marisa had found a scholarship that she could earn, and that had secured admission into a special school in Houston. Including living expenses as well as tuition and other educational costs, that had allowed her to further her training while absorbing scholastic courses that would never have been available in her small home town.

She sighed, half waking, and turned awkwardly onto her side. She sank again into dream, this time dancing, moving to Mozart and feeling the stretch of muscles, the tensions and releases, the brief suspension in space as she leaped into a *grand jeté*.

Multiple layerings of her skirt drifted about her legs, and she knew the familiar pain of the toe-shoes, as well as the pressure of the ribbons about her ankles. The music rose in volume, carrying her back through the years, into a time when her body was young, pliant, and painless. The watchful self that oversaw her sleep understood that this could not last. It warned her not to be sickened when she woke to find herself again in that pile of dying flesh. But she ignored it, burrowing deeper into her dream.

She leaped, high and far—and she was on a country path leading up a hill and into a wood. Barefoot, now, she ran upward, scuffing hot sand between her toes and feeling the talc-fine powder in her nose and throat.

Her grandfather's Jersey cows raised their heads from the lush clover to watch her pass. Henry, the bull, grumbled deep in his chest, but she knew he didn't really mean it. He was the protector of the herd, and she had never feared him.

Then she ran beneath the first trees, and the dust was as cool as it had been warm out in the sun. Big sweet gums arched branches over the trail, which was still rutted deeply by last winter's rains. The track went downhill, winding between hickories and huckleberry bushes and Spanish mulberry.

She paused before moving down that path. A deep breath brought into her lungs the wonderful scent of East Texas woods. The faint sweetness of huckleberry blossoms mingled with the fragrance of the young leaves and the rich aroma of the leaf-mould that was layered beneath the trees. Never, no matter where she went, had that scent been forgotten.

Intoxicated, she stood on tiptoe and whirled like a small tornado, stirring the potpourri of odors about her. Then she ran forward, down the hill, leaping lightly over the worst ruts.

A rabbit scuttered into the brush. A coachwhip snake writhed away beneath a chunk of rock. She sprang over a terrapin that had paused, stunned, in the middle of the track. She danced around the last bend in the trail.

Beyond the screen of hawthorns lay a small pond, mirroring the spring sky. Beyond that again lay the hayfield, lush with flowering vetch and white Dutch clover and rampant Bermuda grass. She would run, just once more, through that field....

But when she dashed forward, it was into her childhood room. The big four-poster, with its cannonball-topped posts, stood solidly in the middle of the wall, waiting for her. Her rag doll, wearing one of her baby dresses, sat on the bed. In its lap purred a kitten.

"Berry!"

The kitten lifted a paw and licked it thoughtfully. Then it rose and rubbed itself beneath the doll's chin, purring loudly.

She laughed. The sound woke her, and she stared up into the darkness of the strange room. A shaft of light arced across the ceiling as a car passed along the road outside, and she sighed, still feeling something of the vigor of that strong young body.

Cornelia closed her eyes again, determined to find that young self again. She dozed....

She faced Aunt Emily across her mother's teakwood table. She was leaning forward, knuckles pressed hard against the black wood. She braced one knee against the curve of the leg, carved in the shape of an elephant's trunk, and felt the tiny ivory tusks hard against her thigh. The pain gave her a strange comfort.

"My mother would tell me to go. She helped me go to school, don't you remember? She wanted me to dance because she said she had always wanted to dance, herself!" She could hear her own voice, light and young.

Emily was sitting in the rocking chair that had been Mom's. That was bad enough. Her face was scarlet, which was always a bad sign, and her hands knitted with awful speed at her interminable purple afghan.

Mom had been bright and full of laughter. Her ambitions had been as unorthodox as her opinions, and if Cornelia had decided to become a combat pilot Mom would have done everything she could to help her do it.

Mom had danced all her life, just for the joy of living, and she knew the frustration of lacking the right training. She

29

understood just where her daughter had gotten her driving need to dance.

Emily was as different from her sister as it was possible to be. She trimmed her sails to the winds of "What will people think?" She feared any ambition more complex than keeping a tidy house with every cell of fat in her rotund body.

"Girls have to get married," she was saying in that overly sweet voice that set Cornelia's teeth on edge. "Once you have a man of your own and a home and some children, all this business about dancing will be forgotten. Girls don't need careers—plain foolishness!" Even thirty years ago, Emily had been behind the times. Girls were becoming doctors and lawyers and anything else they could imagine, though not in the numbers they were now.

What Cornelia had been offered was something so amazing that she never dreamed it might be possible: A full scholarship to a university with a superlative dance department.

That carried with it the opportunity to dance with a small but prestigious company in New York as a member of its tiny corps de ballet. It was a first step, leading to possibilities that would never come again.

"I am going," Cornelia said. She felt choked, but she got the words out. "This is something that I can't refuse. Dance isn't something that you can set aside while you raise a family and then go back to—like school teaching. When your body goes, it's gone forever.

"I am at the right age. I have sound training behind me. I have the credits and the grades to make it at the university, and it won't cost Dad one red cent."

"Well thank heaven for that!" Emily turned even redder. "Folly is bad enough, but expensive folly is the worst. I know what sort of life ballet girls lead. I'm no fool, whatever you may think. You'll come trailing home, pregnant, like as not, and we'll all be disgraced!"

There was no point in arguing with her. Cornelia knew that, for she had had the same sort of dialogue with Coral. Though what business it was of an eleven-year-old she had never figured out.

Dad hadn't wanted to lose her, but he knew his daughter too well to try stopping her. Feet that had been put down had been known to be flattened under the weight of Cornelia's determination. And Eric was solidly behind her, though he had never said much to anyone about that.

He loaned her the fifteen dollars with which she left home. Emily had managed, somehow, to keep Dad from doing anything but providing the train ticket and his blessings, but that had been enough for Cornelia. If Emily thought lack of money would stop her, she was crazy.

She smiled in her sleep. That had been the beginning of her life. She returned home only twice since, once to go to her father's funeral. Her sleeping mind shrank from that memory.

She was standing in the cool marble halls of her first art museum, staring at a painting. A lane wound away between two rows of pollarded trees. The hump of an earth-colored tile roof showed beyond a rise in the ground, where the track curved out of sight.

That had been the moment when she acquired her passion for a particular sort of art. She spoke at once with the docent about the artist, who was long dead.

"Others do similar work," the tiny woman said. "Landscape is always popular." She had found names and addresses there, and later she had followed them up.

Roads—she loved them. That path up the hill into the wood on her family's farm had been the first, she now thought, to gain her heart. There had been many others:

The long double strand of steel rails that took her away from the woods and hills of East Texas. The mazes of British roads that led to unexpected and enchanted corners still holding the past. Bits of Roman road she had seen on her tours in France and Britain.

And now a road stretched before her. Its pavement—or was it gravel?—gleamed with bone-like paleness beneath a half moon. Darkness lay on either hand and beyond the range of vision, yet she could smell the woods scent again, almost as intensely as before.

The darkness was a friendly one. Warm air moved gently against her face, as she moved forward. Something waited beyond the curve ahead.

Masses of scented shrubbery made a wall to her right. She smelled roses and honeysuckle. Intoxicated again, she went onto her toes and spun, arms out, feeling the blood heavy in the tips of her fingers. Then she went toward the waiting—what?—around the curve of the road, and woke.

The luminous dial of the bedside clock told her it was three o'clock. She was thirsty, and she had no intention of waking Amanda to get water.

Without turning on a light, she struggled to sit and pushed her swollen feet off the bed and onto the floor. There was starlight from the window, lighting her way as she moved to the bathroom.

She could still walk, at times, though the effort made her waterlogged heart labor too hard. Once she had her water, she found herself hungry. She had been too weary to eat Cynthia's sandwiches.

Could she make it to the kitchen? Eric wouldn't mind, and she didn't give a damn whether her sister-in-law did or not.

Cornelia felt for her robe, put it on, and slipped out into the hall, setting her feet carefully. Once in the kitchen, she closed the door, to keep the light from waking anyone, and looked into the refrigerator.

Cheese. That would be nice. Lettuce from the crisper, a ripe tomato from a wire container. No better sandwich existed. She was putting the finishing touches to it when the door opened. Eric's tousled gray head came into view.

She smiled and cut another slice of cheese. As she slathered mayonnaise onto bread, she thought of something. "Do you remember Mom's homemade mayo?"

Eric grinned and plopped onto a bar stool. "I have her recipe and her jar with the beater. Once in a while, I make up a batch, but it never tastes quite like hers. Cyn thinks it's uncivilized to make your own mayo, but I do it anyway. When the tomato crop is at its peak and you can get vine-ripened ones for sandwiches, it's uncivilized not to."

They sat and munched quietly, and when the last crust was gone they smiled at each other. They had never been demonstrative, but their affection went deep. Cornelia felt warm all through herself, just being here with her brother again.

"We must go tomorrow," she said. "I know it makes problems for you, having us here. Amos has the house ready, I know, and tomorrow will be the time.

"The wonderful dreams I have had tonight should perk me up enough to make it home without any trouble. Then when Cyn gets on your nerves you can come to me, instead of going to Rome or Paris. We can talk for days, until you are ready to go home again."

"She isn't a bad person," Eric said. "She seems to put on her worst face when she's with you." He laid his hand over hers on the countertop.

"Somehow you always brought out the worst in her, without doing anything to deserve it. You never were sharp with her, and God knows I have seen you cut people off at the knees, when you got mad. When she went on a tear you always very nobly kept your mouth shut.

"It's chemistry, I suppose. Or..."—his gray eyes, a match for her own, narrowed as he pursued his thought—"...it may be because you went out and did something of your own.

"She never has done anything except the woman things she was brought up to think were the only proper activities for a girl. Your success may rankle with her, do you think?"

Cornelia began a nod of agreement, but her soggy heart gave a hard twinge. She felt herself going even paler than her normal doughy hue.

"Back...to bed!" she gasped. "Help me, Eric!"

He half lifted her and took her back along the hall to her room.

Propping her against the pillows, he pulled up the light coverlet and stood beside her. He looked worried, and she took his hand.

"It's just the long trip and the walk to the kitchen. Give me one of those tablets, and I'll be fine in the morning."

"Liar," he said, his tone almost inaudible.

"As fine as a dying woman can be," she replied. "Now go and get some rest. And don't worry! It won't do a bit of good."

He went, but she knew that he lay awake in the night, worrying anyway.

CHAPTER FOUR

A SHORT TRIP HOME

She was, as she promised, better in the morning. Although Eric protested and even Cynthia seemed concerned about what people might think when her ailing sister-in-law left after such a short visit, Cornelia was determined to go home. Eric, of course, insisted on taking her there in his van, saving Amos the drive to town.

Although she didn't mention it, one of the principal reasons for her haste was her desire to get out of town before Coral could come to visit her. Her best relationship with her sister was one undertaken at a distance, she had found over the years.

Eric put her in one of the swiveling seats, strapped firmly with seat belts, so that she could see out. She resisted his efforts to get her to lie down on the couch that was a part of the fittings of the van.

"I will never see this country again," she told him. "I want to see the pine trees and cows grazing in pastures and buzzards circling in the sky. I want to look deep into the woods, as we pass, to see if the dogwoods still show some blossom. You know that I'll never travel this road again."

He had no answer for that. So she watched the tender green of spring leaves slipping past. Eric lowered the windows at her request, and she was able to smell those East Texas woods. The rich, sweet scent put new life into her, as they drove.

As they sped down the highway toward their old home, Cornelia soaked in the feel of her native land. She wished, looking into the vine-cloaked patches of woods, that she could go quietly into the trees and lie down on that smooth mat of pine needles. It would be good to die there, surrounded by growing things that would be nourished by her body.

"I wouldn't even mind the buzzards...," she murmured to herself.

Eric's ears were still sharp. His mind was still, after all the intervening years, attuned to hers. "You always were a maverick," he said over his shoulder. "If the law allowed it, I'd lay you out under the trees, once you are gone, and let the forest take you."

She laughed, feeling her lungs labor. She had missed having someone about her who understood instantly, even her most ridiculous thoughts. Nobody in all her experience had ever measured up to the rapport she shared with her brother.

David least of all! He had not understood what such a thing might be.

They turned off the state highway onto the blacktop running past the family farm. She had bought her sister's share, when her father died.

She had never been able to get Eric to accept any financial help from her, even when his business was very new and shaky. At that point, she had insisted on paying him top dollar for his part of the farm.

For once, he had accepted her offer, and it had been that capital that pulled his business through a difficult time and set it on the road to prosperity.

Now the farm was entirely hers. Emily had, of course, kicked up a fuss, for she had kept house for her brother-in-law after Mom died and had fully expected to come into a share in the property. She ran things with an iron hand for years, and she had expected to continue doing that after Andrew was gone.

It had been a bitter blow to her aunt, Cornelia knew, when, far from returning home broke and pregnant, she had made steady gains in her work. First as a soloist and then as a featured dancer, she had progressed.

36

At last she became prima ballerina of a major company, and as soon as she was making good money she retained Lucius to manage her finances. His wise investments had paid off many-fold.

Before she was thirty, Cornelia was what in East Texas could be called a wealthy woman. Even in New York, she was more than comfortably situated, and as her reputation grew, so did her investments and her income.

When she bought the farm, Emily was devastated. The letter her aunt sent her still rankled, for it accused her of being a high-priced whore, among even more insulting comments.

She had struggled with herself, knowing the limited education and background of her aunt. In Emily's mind, the only way for a woman to make money was as a teacher, a nurse, or a prostitute. But now she wondered if a part of the problem might not be rooted in the thing Eric had mentioned.

A woman who had been trained all her life to be dependent on a man must feel terribly resentful of one who went out in the teeth of all the odds and made it for herself in this new world. Self discipline and strength of purpose were things that Emily had tried to crush out of both her nieces.

She had succeeded with Coral, but Cornelia had been a burr under her saddle since the day her mother died.

Cornelia stared out of the window, shaking off that memory. Inside her mind she composed her own funeral as she would love to arrange it. A bier like Snow White's, without the crystal lid, would be carried into the woods by six men and set onto the pine needles. The body would be removed and laid on the ground.

The weeping relatives (Emily always wept, even if she hated the corpse bitterly) withdrew quietly to leave the remains to the tender mercies of nature. What a scandal that would be! How mortified Emily would feel! She almost laughed.

The van slowed again. They turned off the hard-top onto a graveled road. So many turns; so many roads. She hadn't quite realized how many lay between the town and her old home. Familiarity had blurred them, she supposed.

Now the van rocked with the undulations of the rutted road. Even covered with gravel, the mix of sand and clay in the soil softened in the winter rains. The road machines had not yet smoothed the surface.

Walls of greenery rose on either side of the narrow way. Honeysuckle perfumed the air, its trailers woven into the tangle of elm saplings, sweet gums, tallow trees, and rattan vine.

Beyond the wall on the left there was forest. On the right, occasional glints of reflected light showed from a small lake.

"Is the cougar still in the woods?" she asked suddenly.

"I suspect one of her grandchildren is," her brother said. "He makes his round of the territory about every six months and the cows have hysterics, or somebody sees a track. We don't mention it—some macho idiot would go out and try to shoot him.

"I like to know he's out there, tending to his business, along with the bobcats and the few black bears that are left. Down here near the river it's wild enough to let them keep out of sight and survive."

She sighed with pleasure. "I am so glad you kept things going for me, with the farm. Amos is a good worker, but you told him what to do, and he needs that."

"I'm just glad that the place will stay in the family. I always want to be able to come out here, when things get tense at work, and just let the woods cure me of all my troubles. If only Lisa...."

"I have it arranged so she can't sell it," Cornelia said. "She is young, and Cynthia is her mother. She can't help being what she is, so I gave her some help in the terms of the trust. I hope that one day she'll be glad of it, and if not I'll be gone and won't give a damn."

Eric chuckled. He turned the van into a break in the wall of green and drove up a long drive lined with oak and ash and sweet gum trees, at whose feet bloomed rows of white and scarlet amaryllis.

Beyond, Cornelia could see the fruit trees her father had planted when she was a child, old ones, now, some still showing a trace of spring blossom.

38

The house, strangely enough, had not shrunk, as places usually do that you recall from childhood. It was a big frame house, and the cypress from which their grandfather had built it had hardened to the consistency of iron. The tin roof, kept painted, would outlast all of them, Cornelia knew. Only the porches, which had been built of pine, ever needed replacement.

The last replacement had been a few years past, and Eric had put up decorative metal grillwork as trim. Amos's scarlet climbing roses now ran up the lacy posts and had woven themselves into the pattern, framing the porch.

"A rose-covered cottage!" Cornelia was amused. "Never would I have thought I'd end my days in one!"

But inside it was the same. The one constant in a chaotic world, its shadowy rooms still held the worn reproduction Persian rugs that had been her grandmother's. The pine floors glowed with generations of wax. The Boston fern that Cornelia's mother started fifty years ago had outgrown a sequence of pots and was now ensconced in a huge tub with its own rollers. The mahogany furniture had darkened with age, but it fitted its setting comfortably.

When Eric rolled his sister into the bedroom Ella had prepared for her, she began gasping with laughter. "When I was five, I would have killed to sleep in the Monster Bed," she said. "And now here I am to die in it, instead."

The Broken Star quilt that her grandmother made covered the mattress. The tall headboard, topped with a mahogany gargoyle, seemed to lean forward in welcome.

She looked about at the familiar room, the welcoming bed, already turned back. But she didn't want to rest. She wanted to see everything at once, and over the protests of her brother and Amanda she did just that.

The afternoon sped past. She was weary, and yet it was a different sort from the exhaustion she had known in her city apartment.

The air moved freely through the house, scented with wild growing things. The high ceilings made the rooms cool, and she suspected that the air conditioners Eric had installed would go unused, except when the weather turned unbearably hot.

She was welcomed by Amos, who was no longer the boy she remembered but a middle-aged man, and his wife. Ella was a good match for the big, slow-moving fellow. Small and bright-eyed and brisk, she was just the right balance wheel for him, and she seemed genuinely glad of the opportunity to take on the care of the house.

Amanda took to them both, and that was a relief. The Conwells had never been farther from home than Houston, while the older woman had traveled the world many times over, both as wardrobe-mistress and Cornelia's companion. Still, the three seemed to be compatible in their aim to make life cheerful for their patient.

Cornelia was shown the chickens, the German shepherd who kept away night-prowling varmints, and the herd of beef cattle, grazing across the fishpond on the slope of her remembered hill.

She should have been exhausted. She should have been breathless, in pain from her sluggish heart. Instead, she felt better than she had in months.

She ate a big supper, in comparison with her usual meals. She even found the energy to sit for a time on the porch, as the evening cooled, watching fireflies begin their displays.

A whippoorwill muttered to itself in one of the huge oaks that leaned over the house. When Amanda hauled her off to bed, it was almost eleven, later than she had stayed awake for a very long time.

"I was afraid this was going to be a big mistake," said Amanda as she helped Cornelia from the shower and into her night-dress. "Seemed to me, the sensible thing was to stay in the city where the best doctors are at hand. I couldn't understand why you'd want to go way off to the back of beyond to spend the time left."

She brushed her hair and tied it up with a ribbon. "But now I know. You'll live twice as long here as you'd ever want to, back in the city. How was it you ever left, anyway?"

Cornelia smiled up at her. Amanda grinned back. "I know, I know. I've lived around dancers for most of my life, and nobody knows better the pressure they have inside them to dance. You, too, more than anybody else I've known. There was nothing else for you. Literally.

"I used to wonder why you didn't marry young Timothy—you remember him? The blond who could make Nijinsky look earthbound. But I knew, deep down. You hadn't energy to do anything but dance."

"I do like people who answer their own questions," said Cornelia. "It saves me such a lot of breath."

Amanda turned the ceiling fan to low. "You call if you need me!" Her tone was brusque, but her eyes were filled with affection.

But Cornelia knew that tonight, if never again, she would sleep soundly and need nothing but what she had about her.

Chapter Five

Trek Along a Track

When Cornelia woke it was to the smell of frying bacon and hot biscuits. Her diet, she decided, wasn't ever going to do her any good, and she might as well eat what she liked, when she managed to eat at all. Ella evidently took her statement literally.

Amanda helped her to dress and brushed her hair, yawning constantly. "Don't tell me you couldn't sleep!" said Cornelia.

"Too damn quiet! I kept listening for sirens and traffic noise, and all I could hear was ten million squeaks and croaks and chirrups and what-not. It's going to take some getting used to, I can guarantee."

She eased Cornelia into her chair and pushed it into the wide hall that cut the house in two down the middle. A draught of cool air was always to be found there, pulled between the double doors at the front and the screened porch at the back.

"If breakfast tastes like it smells," Amanda said, sniffing appreciatively, "I can get used to a lot of things."

It did. Cornelia ate as she had not been able to for months. Not much, for her stomach had shrunk, but with enjoyment, which she had thought forever lost. Biscuit and butter and homemade blackberry jam took on new meanings. And everything stayed down.

That gave her the nerve to tackle a duty she didn't dare to put off. "Amos, take me over to the family plot. I want to show you what I want, when I die."

He glanced down at his knobby hands, burnt dark by the scorching suns of forty summers. "Miss Cornelia, I hate to think about that. Why don't you just write it down, and we'll tend to things when the time comes?"

"I want to do it this way," she said. "I feel up to going, this morning, and from past experience I know I may never feel like it again. So get out the pickup and help me in. We can put the chair in the back, so Amanda can squeeze in, too."

The ride was familiar, but so many years had passed that she felt as if she were going backward in time. Her first visit here had been at the burial of her great aunt Rosemary.

She'd been perhaps four or five, and Mom had let her attend her first funeral, as there would be small cousins there to distract her from the sadness of the occasion.

They had, too. She didn't recall much about the funeral except the games of hide and seek in the woods about and among the gray-lichened headstones.

Amos drove along an overgrown track, deep into the wood. The family had established its own burial ground when the first Watson died on his land grant, far back when Texas was a Republic. Now some fifteen of his descendants lay there, with wives or husbands or children, their markers in varying states of tilt and sag.

The pickup moved down the sandy lane, the huckleberries on either side scraping the metal. Wild rose vines' draped tendrils slithered over the top of the cab. Great pines, bigger even than those near the house, loomed like a thick green ceiling, hiding the sky.

Cornelia felt a catch in her chest—not her heart but a memory. Something about the darkness beneath the trees had always made her feel obscurely uneasy. Crossing the River Jordan, as the spirituals called it, might be something like this. The Watson family cemetery was like a remote antechamber of the sort of Underworld in which the Greeks had believed.

Amos helped her into her chair, and Amanda went ahead to open the gate. They went through it into a stillness that filled the small area inside the tight metal fence.

Nobody spoke. Cornelia couldn't even hear her companions breathing, for her heart thudded loudly. Only a light breeze moved, whispering in the tops of the pines, and a mockingbird, strangely silent, watched them with bright and secretive eyes from his perch on the fence.

A tiny patch of sunlight found its way through the canopy to touch her mother's headstone. A coachwhip, coiled on the grassy mound, lowered its head and slid behind the marker.

Cornelia shook herself. "I want my ashes put into a jar of some kind and buried between Mom and Dad. It won't take much digging—you can do it with a trowel. Roll me closer, so I can show you where."

The chair bumped over the rough grass to the spot she indicated. "Be sure you don't cut the roots of the white rose. But get as near as you can, and leave the top off the jar, so I can fertilize the roses." She gazed down at the mounds beneath which lay her parents.

Beyond her mother's was a tiny one, where a stillborn brother lay. She had not been born, when he came and went. Eric had come next, then she had been born, with Coral coming last.

"I wonder if Eric and Coral...." She caught herself. "Of course not. Cynthia already has a plot in the new cemetery in town. On the ritzy end.

"Coral will go where her husband's family is buried. And if Aunt Emily tries to get herself in here, I'll rise up and haunt her myself!"

She looked up at Amanda. "Remind me to write it into my will as a codicil. Emily Stillson is expressly forbidden burial in the Watson plot. She made trouble for Mom all their lives, and she drove my Dad to an early grave, I feel certain, with her nagging and her managing."

She drew a deep breath, suppressing the cough that always followed. "There's a lot to be said for owning the land and the plot."

Amanda cleared her throat. "You know, C'nelia, I never put much faith in the tales I've heard about old graveyards and ghosts and such, but if ever there was a place where you might find such things, this is it. If you've done, I'd much appreciate getting my tail out of here.

"Besides, it's chilly, here in the deep shade. You don't want to catch cold."

Cornelia shivered. She, too, had found the old graveyard forbidding. Strange to think that her ashes would be here, in a very short while. Forever. Somehow, that didn't bother her; it seemed fitting.

"Amos, see if you can get someone to come in and cut the grass and trim the shrubbery. I don't want anybody getting wasp-stung when they come to my funeral. I think I see a wasp-nest in that cape jasmine bush over there. Does Bud Miller still have a lot of sons at home? They used to do such work."

Amos turned the chair toward the gate. "Nowadays his boys don't work. They sit home and drink beer and dope themselves out of their gourds. Or else they go out and knock over tombstones for a pastime. You don't want them to come back here.

"Likely they don't know it's here, or they would have paid it a visit already. No, I'll get around to it. I kind of like it, to tell the truth." He waited while Amanda closed the gate and fastened the padlock he had produced from the pocket of the pickup.

"I don't suppose you'd have room for Ella and me, when the time comes?" he murmured. He lifted her into the pickup and set the chair in the bed.

Cornelia was feeling the effects of the outing, now. Her heart was slogging on its way, but her entire body felt weak. When she pulled herself together a bit, she turned to look at Amos, who was backing the pickup and turning into the track along which they had come.

"I don't see why not. There's plenty of space, and I can't see any more Watsons wanting to be buried back here. They were optimistic when they enclosed the place—we've never been a prolific bunch.

"So I'll put you and Ella in when I make sure Emily is out. It's the least I can do, after the way you have cared for the place since Dad died."

He didn't speak, but a smile lightened his weathered face. "Miss Emily won't be happy about it, us being in and her out," he said. His eyes were full of laughter. "She don't hold with consorting with the help. Told me so herself, the day your Dad died."

"Precious little consorting we'll do after we're dead," Cornelia said. "But what there is, we'll do. I expect to hear from Emily about it, if she has to chase me through the Hereafter to give me a piece of her mind."

Amanda handed her a tablet from the vial she carried in her pocket. "You take one of these. You sound like a pipe organ that's almost out of air. Never should have let you come on this expedition to begin with! You didn't need this kind of exertion, and when we get back you're going to drink a cup of soup and go to bed."

Cornelia had known she would have to pay for the outing. She wasn't surprised when Amanda's prescription wasn't enough to stave off the reckoning. For three days she was flat on her back, or as flat as she could be and still breathe. Time flowed over her like water over a stone, leaving no impression on her mind.

What brought her to herself again was the prick of a needle in her arm.

"You give me any painkiller, and I'll rise up and flatten you," she muttered, still only half aware.

She opened her eyes to see someone—obviously a doctor, though a very young one—bending over her. He let out a yelp of laughter.

"They told me you were feisty. They warned me you don't live by their rules and probably would shoot me on sight, but I came anyway, when your companion called.

"I had to meet Cornelia Watson while I could. I have seen every film ever made of your work." His brown eyes crinkled at the corners, and she found herself smiling up at him.

"Then you understand why I have no objection to dying," she said.

He sat in the low rocker beside the bed and nodded. "I understand. It's contrary to everything I was taught in medical school, but if I had to live with your physical problems I probably would want to let go, too.

"The congestive heart failure isn't enough. No, you had to develop kidney problems, as well. I know how you must feel, and I know your brother. You're a lot alike."

She sighed with relief. "You mean that I am not going to have to fight you down to the wire to stop you from trying to save my life? You're not going to have me declared mentally incompetent because I want to end this torture whenever nature lets me go?"

"Hey!" He looked alarmed and concerned. "I came because your friend Amanda said you needed some help. You were having trouble breathing and she thought you were in pain. And you were, even semi-conscious, weren't you?"

"Well...yes. But I'm used to it. And it will be over before long, one way or another."

"But why hurt? I can, I think, make your last days more comfortable, without drugging you out of your mind."

She tried to sit, failed, and accepted his hand to help her higher on the pillows. "Do you mean that? You can give me something that will help without putting me out into left field?"

"Let me try. If it doesn't work to your satisfaction, I'll stop. And let me visit you from time to time. I want to see those paintings Amanda told me about."

The shot was already helping, and she breathed with less effort. The dull pain all over her body had subsided to an endurable level.

"Feel free. I don't really hate doctors, you know. Just the members who try to make me conform to their ideas of proper behavior for dying people. Same goes for just about everyone else.

"Amanda, my brother, and the Conwells just about make up my list of friends, now. I'll be glad to add you to it. It has become rather short."

Amanda entered with a cup of broth. "You haven't eaten enough to keep you alive, these past few days. Drink this.

"Jonathan is going to visit me, whether you let him come to see you or not. I've taken a fancy to him, and I'd set my cap for him if he wasn't married."

Cornelia accepted the cup and took a sip. "You don't have to sneak him in. I like him. We'll let him be our token medic, just to keep Emily and Cynthia and Coral off our necks."

She finished off the broth and set the cup aside. "I take it that you might be willing to become my defense against well-meaning relatives?"

"Glad to. I am, by the way, Jonathan Williamson. And I'd love to take a look at those paintings, if you don't mind. I am an art fanatic."

She nodded. "Take him into the living room, Amanda, and show him. I want Amos to bring them in here, one at a time, so I can study them while I lie in bed. Meanwhile, we can leave the rest where they are.

"Turn on the lights, so he can see them easily. I will be interested to know what you think of them," she said to the doctor.

When they returned, Jonathan looked dazed. "Your mother was bitten by a road?" he asked. "I never dreamed there were so many kinds of paintings of thoroughfares, paths, lanes, highways, and country roads! What beautiful work!"

She smiled. "They are all the roads I had no time or energy to follow. My life was concentrated along one route, and all the side-roads had to be passed by.

"I knew I was missing many important things, and I yearned to know what lay beyond the bends or over the hills, but I had no time to go. So I bought representations, large and small, to be enjoyed in my old age." She gave a sound between cough and laugh.

"But I don't consider it a waste. This will comfort my death, and the museum will be happy to have them back. Others will enjoy them for generations, I hope."

He took her hand. "A fine investment. I envy you your journeys down those paths."

"I will leave one to you! Come back often to study them. Choose the one you like best, and it will be my thank-you for keeping an old woman company."

"Old woman? You are Cornelia Watson, the greatest dancer of our age. It's a privilege to help you along, but I must admit that I would love to have one of your paintings. I'll choose carefully.

"But now I must go. An overdue infant is probably about to come into the world, and I need to check on its mother. I will come later, if I may."

Amanda returned from seeing him off, a packet in her hand. "He left some tablets, so you won't have to suffer when it gets bad. But you'd better rest again. You're looking pale."

Cornelia had to agree. But she lay for a long time against her pillows, thinking about Jonathan Williamson. It had been a long while since she had made a new friend. All the old ones had fled from her illness, and it was good to find one who wasn't afraid to be close to someone who was dying.

Tomorrow, she would have Amos bring in a painting and hang it opposite her bed, above the marble topped table, in place of the mirror. Instead of seeing a reflection of dissolution, she would find possibilities she had never had time to explore.

It would make things much easier.

CHAPTER SIX

AN ATTACK OF EMILY

A painting was hung the next day, on the wall beyond the foot of the Monster Bed. Cornelia chose, for the first, a wagon track through pine trees, with low-growing ferns and woodland flowers in the foreground. It rested her to look at it as she lay on her pillows.

She was more exhausted every day, and lying in bed studying a landscape was just about all she could manage. Her medication, true to Jonathan's promise, didn't send her into orbit.

Instead, it soothed the pain to a bearable level, and it also produced a feeling of quiet reflection that sometimes led to almost metaphysical moods. She had never had the time for such thoughts, and she enjoyed the odd notions that came to her, now.

She had been given a tablet and now lay quietly, staring up that wagon track. She was almost able to see around the bend, when Amanda entered her room, her face a map of dismay.

"Your Aunt Emily is in the living room. She says that if she is not allowed to see you she will go to the sheriff and get him to send out a deputy to make sure you are alive and able to make your own decisions.

"She thinks the Conwells and I are robbing you blind, while letting you lie in your own filth. Of course, I gave as good as I got, but I see what you mean about her. She can shut up her ears like a hippopotamus."

Cornelia groaned. "If I refuse to see her, she's capable of doing just that. So tell her she can come in for a moment, but you stay in your room with the door open. I want to have help at hand. Not to protect me—to protect her. If anyone alive could make me rise from this bed and strangle her, it's Emily."

She smoothed her hair and pulled the coverlet straight. The sound of Emily's fat feet pattering on her hardwood hall floor set her teeth on edge, and she didn't even try to smile. It was all she could do to keep from frowning ferociously.

Emily looked about the sunny room, her small brown eyes checking everything in quick, darting glances. The tranquility of the room, the spotless bed linen, the composed attitude of her niece seemed to irritate her severely.

"Well, I expected to find you looking even worse. They tell me you're dying. Are you?"

That was Emily. She trampled over people's feelings without remorse or even awareness, but let someone hint at a slight or a snub toward her, and she was loudly devastated.

Cornelia kept her calm. She held her hands still on the folded-back sheet in her lap, controlling the urge to throw a pillow at her aunt. "I am dying, if that gives you any pleasure. I am swollen and uncomfortable, but I am quite alert and fully capable of controlling my own life, such as it is. I always have been, if you remember."

Emily plumped down into the low rocker by the bed. She took out that hideous purple afghan, which either had been ripped out every night, to be worked on, Penelope-like, for forty years or else was one of an endless number done in identical shades and pattern. She thumped her knitting bag onto the floor and began to work the needles. "You never were a dutiful girl. Never a lady! Gave me fits; when you refused Harold Montgomery's offer before you went off to college I just never forgave you. You were never..."—she fixed an agate eye on Cornelia—"...one to concern yourself with what people would think."

Cornelia found a laugh bubbling up. "I haven't changed a jot. Now what is it that brings you here? Not affection—spare me protestations of family love. We never pretended that, even before Mom died.

"No, I suspect you are in that chair because someone at church asked if you had visited me yet, and you are worried about what they thought when you said no. Right?"

The needles clicked nervously, as Emily squirmed in the rocker. She set her feet flat on the floor and pushed the chair back and forth with petulant jerks. "You are my sister's oldest daughter. My own flesh and blood. Of course I came to see you! Why must you be so ugly about things?"

"Oh, my God! Emily, being honest is not a synonym for being ugly. I hate your guts. You hate mine. Do admit that, for once, and then tell me what it is that you want."

The round face was a mottled scarlet. "If you have to make it so sharp, I have come to make you see the light. About Coral. About making your peace with God.

"After the loose life you've led, I know it's time you gave some thought to such things. You haven't, I feel sure. You never darkened the church door unless I forced you to."

Cornelia looked past her aunt into the peaceful wood of the painting. "Do you honestly think that I could have worked as hard as I did, putting every ounce of energy I possessed into making my inner truth visible to others, without being at peace with both God and myself?

"If you think I have lived a loose life, it proves that you know nothing about me. If I recall, you raked me over the coals when I was fourteen, because I refused to date any of the boys in school."

Emily avoided that in her usual manner, by shifting the subject. "You must see Coral. She's grieving about your un-Christian attitude toward her." She rocked harder, and the afghan flapped its purple wings on her lap.

What a nasty situation! Cornelia tried to relax, to sound reasonable instead of angry. "Coral has never liked me. I consider her shallow and insincere. And, Emily, there are a lot more truths than you have ever found in the Fairfield Methodist Church!"

"I am sending Brother Pierce to see you tomorrow!" her aunt squeaked. "I never heard such blasphemy! Other truths—he'll soon set you straight.

"And poor little Coral's grieving because she can't visit her only sister. It's a pure sin, Cornelia. You always harden your heart, just like the Pharaoh."

"If Coral really wants to see me, tell her she can come. Once. For a very short visit. If she will be civil, fine. But if she begins her usual ranting, out she goes. Amanda can handle her with one hand. Now it's time for you to go, too." Cornelia felt as if she had run a mile, and her heart sloshed heavily in her chest.

There was an outraged expression on her aunt's red face. "I just got here! I haven't finished the fourth row!"

"You have committed all the rows on that atrocity that will be knitted in my house. You have seen me. You can now go tell your friends that, and if they urge you to come again, lie to them.

"I will not let you in again. I have little enough time left, without its being so unpleasant. I hate to waste it on you or Coral." She leaned even more heavily into the pillows. "Amanda!"

Amanda appeared in the door, as if by magic. "Yes, C'nelia?"

"Please show my aunt out. And bring me some ice. I am overheated."

Emily huffed to her feet, folding the afghan into the knitting bag. "My sister would turn in her grave, if she knew the way you've spoken to me.

"Great dancer! Ha! I know what dancers do, and it isn't dancing. Whoring! You've got a lot to answer for, Cornelia, and I don't envy you when you come face to face with the Almighty!"

Cornelia didn't open her eyes. "Emily, you're all broken out with envy like a case of the hives. Get out of here, or I'll have Amos throw you out onto the lawn."

The fat feet stamped away down the hall. Cornelia felt that Ella might have to sand away the indentations in the polished wood, her heels struck so hard. But maybe this would end it; she hoped never again to see Emily, in this life or any other.

She felt sick and hot, and she was glad when Amanda returned with ice, as well as fresh mint tea. After sucking a sliver of ice, she sipped the tea and felt her nerves settle again.

Amanda said nothing. She sat and drank her own tea in silence. That was the best thing about her; she knew when to speak and when not to.

After a while, Cornelia said, "I wish that I were one of those lovely people who can relate to others on their own level. I wish I could make Emily feel happy and wanted, instead of rejected. I wish I could want to see my only sister. I wish...."

"That you were perfect," Amanda finished for her. "Nobody is. Why worry? Think, instead, about the dancers you helped along the way. The old, sick ones you set up with trust funds to keep them in boarding houses and nursing homes. You didn't fool me for a minute...I saw more than you thought.

"Lucius told me, too. I helped him figure out ways to get the stiff-necked ones to accept help without feeling it was charity. That took some doing, you'd better believe."

Cornelia looked with new respect at her companion. "You are a sharp one, my friend. What would you do about Emily, if you were unfortunate enough to have her in your family?"

"Cuss her out well and truly, then feel like a villain, just the way you do. I'm not as patient as you were. You handled her better than I could have, believe me.

"But that sort of woman wants to be mistreated. It makes her feel important and it gives her something to complain about to other women just like her. Then they all sit around and groan about what the world's coming to, when a Christian woman can be treated so badly."

Cornelia laughed. It hurt, but that was fine, too, for Amanda had seen through her aunt with shrewd understanding. It had taken her minutes to do what had required years for Cornelia to accomplish.

She felt as if she had had a bad attack. Then she realized that she had. An attack of Emily was about as bad as it could get.

CHAPTER SEVEN

A CASE OF CORAL

She knew all too well that if Emily came, Coral would not be far behind. She was relieved that two days separated their visits, though she suspected they had put their heads together, plotting strategies.

Coral came in the morning, for which Cornelia was grateful. She had a bit of energy in the morning.

Amanda showed her sister into the room, and on her wrinkled face was an unidentifiable expression. As she turned to leave, Amanda quirked an eyebrow in her old signal that said, "Watch out! Things are not what they seem."

Cornelia wasn't surprised. Things were seldom what they seemed, with her sister.

Coral was the only brown-eyed child of their parents, which was an odd reversal of the common order of heredity. Hers were not as small as Emily's, but they already were showing traces of sharpness and suspicion. They widened to their limits as she stared at her sister.

It didn't surprise Cornelia. The difference between the lissome young woman she had been and the gross and dying creature she had become was appalling.

Yet she had helped Amanda make her as neat and impressive as possible. Her hair, still chestnut and curly, was smoothed into a crown of braids. Her bed jacket was made of antique French lace.

Her room was immaculate. Plants in the windows added freshness, and it did not look or smell like a sickroom. Books and papers were arranged on the bedside table with the mov-

55

able arm on which she could work. Now it was pushed back, and she laid a hand on it as she waited for her sister to speak.

The gesture attracted Coral's gaze. "What's all that?" She was staring at the neat stacks of manuscript paper and the fat notebooks.

"I am writing a book." That should be a safe subject, as Coral never read one if she could avoid it. "I've known a lot of fascinating people and performed in many countries, in my career. This is a sort of professional autobiography, and a publisher has agreed to buy it."

Coral's expression changed, her eyes narrowed. To her, Cornelia realized, having a book published meant instant wealth, whatever the true economics of the writing life might be. But she was trying to control her instinctive reaction to the scent of money.

"Well, I'm glad you're staying busy. It's much better that way. We've worried about you, Emily and I, and Eric, too, though he doesn't show his feelings. I often wonder if he has any."

Cornelia recognized the thought that Coral left unsaid. She had been accused of having no feelings too often not to.

For some reason, however, Coral was holding herself in check, keeping back all the hurtful things she had become so used to hurling at her sister on the infrequent occasions when they met as adults.

"I hope your husband is well," Cornelia said, hoping this olive branch would keep things pleasant. But communicating with Coral was never easy.

"Fine. But I am devastated about you! Even...." She stopped short.

"Even if I do deserve to suffer because I lived a free and independent life, instead of being tied to a house and a husband as a decent woman should be," Cornelia finished for her.

Coral flushed scarlet. "I didn't say that. You did. Here I am being as nice as I know how, and you keep putting words into my mouth."

Cornelia felt a surge of guilt. Coral was right; so far all the hostility had come from her, not her sister. She smiled and held out a hand.

"I'm sorry. Come sit in the rocker and tell me how the family is getting on. I do care, you know, even if I had to go a long way and suffer a lot to realize it."

After that, Coral was almost too sweet and accommodating. Not a word of criticism passed her lips, though Cornelia saw her bite down on unspoken comments more than once. In order to ease the atmosphere, Cornelia began telling amusing anecdotes about her life as a dancer.

Meetings with prime ministers and rulers of nations didn't seem to impress her at all. But when she began telling about her experiences in Hollywood, as she worked at her brief film career, Coral perked up her ears.

"You mean you know all those actors? In person?"

"I designed the choreography for several musicals, and I danced in three, yes. You get to know people fairly well when you work on a film with them.

"*Dance of the Hours* was a big budget production, and we worked closely with the actors and the director. Those six movies let me meet a lot of people.

"Strange as it may seem, some of them seemed to be a bit in awe of me. There's still a sort of mystique about ballet that impresses those who know about such things."

"So that's where you made all that money!"

Aha! thought Cornelia.

"They paid me well, but I made quite nice sums once I began doing solo work. I put my income into the hands of a financial adviser, who was also my lawyer, and he invested it for me.

"He has done quite well, but unfortunately the old age I thought I was providing for isn't going to happen." She looked up as Amanda brought in fresh coffee and pastries on a silver tray.

"Here, have something. Ella is a marvelous cook!" She leaned back as Coral helped herself.

They chatted for quite some time, after that. It was amazing that they could manage it, after so many years of vituperation, Cornelia thought.

Coral, with her nice sense of timing, interrupted the thought with, "What are you going to do with what money you have left? Even spending a lot, you won't be able to go through it all, I suspect, sick as you are."

So that was it. The object of the entire exercise. Cornelia smiled, now that she understood where things stood. "Lisa will get it. I know that you and Eric are well off. I'd leave it to a snake before Emily would get a dime.

"Lisa is my parents' only grandchild, and she will be my heir. Though she won't get everything at once or without supervision. I know her too well to do that."

"Lisa! Everything?" Coral's voice was sharp.

"Coral, if you need anything, tell me now. I will write you a check for any reasonable amount, here and now, though after the things you and Emily have said to me over the years I'd think you might feel guilty at taking anything from me.

"If you have a need that your husband's income can't meet, I will provide it, if it is within my means. But not in my will. I will be gone, and I have seen too many families torn apart by inheritances."

Coral's face matched her name. She opened her mouth, closed it, opened it again. "I don't mean that I want anything!" she protested. "If anyone got anything, it should be Emily, after the way she cared for Dad. He would have had nobody, without her."

Cornelia rose on the pillows. "She bullyragged and coddled and nagged him to death," she said between her teeth. "He would have lived for years, if he had been able to get out and marry again. But Emily was always going into a decline at the notion.

"She nagged him into a heart attack and then she hurried him into his grave with her sweetness and light. He wrote me often, did you know that?"

Coral shook her head. She was biting the insides of her lips.

"He hated her, but he felt too sorry for her to throw her out. He also told me that our great-grandmother left her well provided for. Did you know that?"

"Mom's mother? No, I never heard that her side of the family had anything at all."

"Emily inherited oil-producing land. Mom gave her share to her sister, trying to keep her up there in Oklahoma tending to her business, but it didn't work.

"Emily could buy up half of East Texas, if she wanted. I had Lucius look into her affairs, years ago. She has interest-bearing accounts and CD's from Beaumont to Tulsa, since she sold her leases at the height of the oil boom."

Amanda brought in fresh coffee. Coral accepted another cup, but she seemed absent-minded. She stirred the sugar in. Then she looked up at Cornelia. "No, I most certainly didn't know that. Emily pretends to be on the edge of starvation. She's always getting little loans from my husband. She pays it back in dribs and drabs, if she pays it back at all. So. She's not as poor as she claims to be...."

"No. Lucius has the proof. She sold off the land and the leases when things were at their peak. The money went into Certificates of Deposit, principally. Don't let her con you."

"The one thing you never did was lie," Coral said. She put her empty cup on the *tabouret*. "At times I've wished you would, just to smooth things over. But I'm glad I came, even if you do look tired. You've given me something to think about."

Listening to Coral's heels tapping lightly down the hall, Cornelia felt that might be true. Now her sister would put her mind toward ways and means of getting her hands on some of Emily's money.

She chuckled. "I sicced her onto Emily," she said, as Amanda came into the room. "Got her off my back for a while."

"I hope so. You told me how she was, and once I met her at the door and saw her, all honey and melted butter, I knew something was afoot.

"That girl was here for a purpose, bound and determined on something. I should have known you'd manage her. Here, let me lower your head so you can sleep a bit."

She lay back on the pillows, exhausted, as she was so often, now. Even with Jonathan's medicine she knew she couldn't endure much.

Amanda closed the blinds, shutting out the sun and the glare from the lawn outside. The painting glowed dimly, the light lending its subtle colors a mystical mood.

Cornelia tried to drift on the tide of the medication, onto that path between the pines. She closed her eyes, visualizing the spot. Concentrating, she relaxed body and mind and put herself outside her normal frame of reference. She smelled pine needles in a summer wood. Ironwort bloomed on either hand, its tall stalks dusty green beneath the fluffs of purple blossom. Spanish mulberry echoed the purple in its berries, and she knew it was fall, there in the painting.

Pale dust curled up beneath her feet, as she moved into the cool shade of the trees. Beside the track, layers of old leaves blanketed the soil.

Seedlings of many kinds sprouted there, most never to reach the sun, roofed as they were with canopies of leaves. But they grew hopefully, along with yellow jasmine vines and Virginia creeper and poison ivy.

She noted everything as she passed, but she kept moving along the track to the bend, at which the perspective of the painting ended. Once she rounded that old obstacle, she paused, staring up in amazement.

Here the trees were tremendous pines, larger than those at the cemetery. The tops rustled with a breeze that couldn't find its gentle way into the lower thicknesses. The boles were many times the girth of her body, shooting up sixty or seventy feet, where they laced brittle arms together in a roof of dark green needles.

The track was almost obscured by the carpet of needles lying beneath the trees. An occasional sweet gum lightened the green above, where single shafts of sunlight struck through.

She turned aside from the path and lay full-length on the pine-needle mat, reveling in the feel of this dream-body that was not ill. The scent of pine straw was intoxicating, and the occasional cone buried in its depths was only an added attraction. This was a place of rest.

The sort of place she had longed for, as she rode home with Eric. This was a spot for dying peacefully and going back to the soil.

What the buzzards and the insects wanted, they could have. The rest could lie, pale and calcified, until time covered it with pine straw and leaves and moss.

Even as she understood that, she heard something in the distance. Something intriguing: she couldn't die until she knew what it might be.

Chapter Eight

The One in the Wood

Cornelia felt herself waking. She struggled to slip back into her deep dream, knowing that she was about to find something wonderful. She put all her will into flowing back into the dark tide of sleep.

Then she found that she had succeeded. The pine wood murmured around her; the pine straw rustled as she turned toward the source of the voice that called through the trees. A mockingbird went through his repertory, unseen in a nearby bush, as she gazed toward the path.

There was a glint of blue—blue jean blue. A flash of yellow gingham shirt, checkered with white. A light footstep and a shrill whistle.

Then a yell—"Horace! Horace, you idiot, don't chase that rabbit! Come here!" echoed through the wood, and a child was there, touched with a ray of sunlight piercing the needled branches far above.

Cornelia sat up and brushed straw from herself. "Hello!" she called.

The child turned, her gray eyes widening as she realized that someone else was in the forest. Then she smiled. There was something strangely familiar about the way her lips curved, her cheeks rounded.

Cornelia couldn't quite identify the resemblance, but she felt oddly at ease with this young one. Children had always made her nervous. This one did not.

"Hi. I'm Elissa Andrews. Who're you?" The voice was clear and low, in contrast to the shrill commands to the dog, which now appeared through a screen of wild gooseberry bushes and proceeded to lick Cornelia's face until she rose in self-defense.

"I'm Cornelia. I love your woods."

Elissa grinned. "It's the best place in the world. I come here when I finish my chores. Daddy doesn't mind as long as I don't neglect anything. Mama comes here, too, when she finds the time."

That strong resemblance to someone she should know returned to Cornelia. Andrews...she had known a Charlie Andrews, back in high school. She'd liked him, and she thought he liked her, though both had been too shy to pursue the matter. This might well be his daughter. The tilt of the eyebrows—not like Charlie, but very like someone....

"Is your Dad Charlie Andrews?"

Elissa plumped herself down onto a fallen log, first checking it for ants. "Yes, he is. The neatest father in the world. He understands things."

Cornelia sighed. "I thought so. I think I went to school with him, long ago. He was quiet, but you felt there were all sorts of interesting things going on inside him."

Elissa grinned even wider. "He makes up games," she said. "And he can build anything. He made us a swing set better than any you could buy. He built a boat for us to paddle around the pond.

"He can fix a doll or a toy train, and he makes popguns out of elderberry shoots. We shoot chinaberries through them."

"He used to win all the spelling matches," Cornelia told her.

"Oh, he beats everybody at Scrabble. Even our teachers, when they come out here to fish."

"That doesn't surprise me."

"They don't mind," said Elissa. "Daddy knows more things without going to college than a lot of people know who've gone all their lives. Miss Harvey told me that, and she ought to know.

"He reads everything. Mama says he could retire if we had all the money he spends on books, but he just laughs.

And she reads them as fast as he does. We all do, and work, and play games, and laugh."

Cornelia felt a pang. What a lovely tribute the child had given her parents without appreciating what a rare thing it was to have such a family.

A whistle rang through the trees, two long notes followed by a short one. "That's Daddy," Elissa said. "Mama's in town, and he fixed lunch today. Come back and eat with us—he always makes more than enough." The child tugged at her hand. "I know he'll like you. You feel like family."

Cornelia allowed Elissa to lead her along the track, deeper into the pines. That warm hand in her own was gritty, pulsing with energy. It felt like a small animal, quick with its own life.

She hadn't held the hand of a child since Coral was small, and she had forgotten the feel of it.

They wandered between the huge pines, around the white oaks. Passing a small glade glowing with clumps of ironwort and goldenrod, they rounded the last bend and saw the sky sweeping away beyond the trees. A meadow dotted with clumps of sweet gum spread out on either hand.

The house was plain and solid, with cape jasmines crouching about its foundation like chicks beneath a hen. Cornelia followed Elissa up the brick path to the screen door, which stood open to reveal a large living room beyond, where a ceiling fan moved lazily, bringing to her nose the scent of frying chicken.

"Neat-o!" Elissa whooped.

Cornelia smiled at the man who now stood in the kitchen door. It was Charlie: older, somewhat gray at the temples and a bit soft at the waist, but still tanned and solid. His blue eyes greeted her, and his smile was just the same.

"Don't I remember you?" he asked. "You do look familiar."

"High school, Class of 1958, if I recall correctly. I am...."—but before she could introduce herself, two small boys came bursting into the room, waving damp hands as they made for the kitchen.

He shrugged and gestured toward the laden table in a window-lined nook. "Come on and eat. I knew you, right off, name or no!"

She detoured past the bathroom to wash up, before following him into the old-fashioned kitchen. The long table stretched along three windows, with another at either end of the nook.

Cornelia took her place at one end, while Charlie sat at the other and said, "I'm sorry my wife isn't here today. She had to see the doctor. We're going to add another to this crew. She's only forty-five, but that is a bit old to have a baby, and they keep a close eye on her."

"You have a wonderful family, Charlie. I envy you—I never married."

He looked sad. "Too bad. Life can be pretty lonely when you haven't anyone to share it. And kids—why I wouldn't know what to do if I didn't have them. They make life...interesting."

He chuckled and served more chicken, green beans, mashed potatoes, and turnips all round.

He was a marvelous cook, she decided. She also noted that the children were well-mannered, though he was nothing but quiet and gentle with them.

He protested when she insisted on helping wash up, but they spent a pleasant fifteen minutes, reminiscing about classmates and teachers from their school days.

Only when she had drafted Elissa to guide her back and was following her along the walk did Cornelia remember that she hadn't ever had the chance to tell Charlie who she was. She didn't know who he had married, either, though he had indicated it was one of their classmates.

She turned and called, "Charlie, who did you marry? I never thought to ask. Did I know her?"

He grinned. "Probably you did. Neely's the one I married. Neely Watson." Then he was gone back into the house, leaving her gasping with shock.

Elissa's hand, warm in her own, faded, evaporating into a faint trace of dampness. She clenched her hand hard, trying to regain the contact, but now it was empty.

And the house—was gone.

She opened her eyes and stared at the painting. A road that she had not taken lay behind its quiet surface. A life she had never led, children she had not borne, a husband she had passed without recognizing him, along the way.

Tears formed in her eyes. Surely, somewhere, Elissa and her brothers had been born. Surely Charlie had married a woman who could make him beam as he had when he mentioned his wife! But she had not been the one.

Had her old focus on her life's work deprived those children of reality?

Surely not. This was only a fever-dream, the product of Jonathan's effective medicine. But she still felt an echo of the warm contentment she had known in that house beyond the painted forest, as well as a thrill of sadness.

What a pity that there was no way to pursue every road you crossed along the way. There were so many things she would have liked to do, as well as the single all-demanding one she had been driven to follow.

She touched the bell, and Amanda appeared.

"You all right?" She stared down at Cornelia. "You look funny. Is there anything I can do?"

"Would you ask Amos to come see me, after supper? I'd like to ask him something," Cornelia murmured.

"Of course. Now it's time to wash up and brush your hair. It's almost six o'clock, and Ella has made some soup that will curl your whiskers."

After supper, Amos came into her room, quiet and shy, and sat in the little rocker. "What can I do for you, Ma'am?" he asked.

"Do you remember a family named Andrews? They had a farm west of town and a son named Charlie. Charles Wesley, I think it was. I went to school with him, and I wondered what has happened to him in the years since I knew him."

Amos concentrated in his slow way. Then he nodded. "Old man Arthur Andrews's family. His boy Ike had two sons. Steve was killed in Vietnam, I think. Regular army, I think he was. His brother was Charlie. Hadn't thought about that boy in years.

"He was a smart fellow, too. Took that old cottoned-out farm and built it up and made it pay. Too bad."

Cornelia felt her chest constrict. "Why too bad?"

"About the time he had the place running fine, cattle getting fat, catfish ponds beginning to pay off, he had a heart attack. Do they call it a coronary occlusion? Something like that. Died, right there in his hayfield.

"He was real young. Mid-twenties, if I recollect right, though I was just a kid at the time. His nephew runs the place now. Good boy, but no Charlie.

"They tore down the old homeplace, and that was a real pity. Charlie loved that house, from what I saw when I helped work the hay there."

"Was it a house in a meadow, beyond a pine woods? Trees all around and roses on the gate?"

Amos looked surprised. "I can hardly remember it myself. You must have visited him there."

Cornelia lay heavily against the pillows. "Yes, I did. I visited him there, I think." I hope, she said inside herself.

Amanda shooed Amos out. "You look ready to drop," she scolded her patient. "It's time you take your medicine and your bath and rest some. You've been having too many visitors for somebody in your shape."

After Amanda finished with her, Cornelia lay quietly, watching the light drain from the sky beyond the window. She didn't turn her eyes toward the painting. She had been down that road, just a bit, and she knew she could not bear another trip.

Had that been a medication-induced dream? Or had she caught a glimpse of an alternative her life might have known, if she'd looked aside from her goals?

And Charlie—if she had encouraged him and he had responded, would he have become the man she had known so briefly? Would he have died early in the hot dust of a hayfield?

She refused to think of Elissa and the boys. Those children were too vital, too warm and alive never to have existed. They must have been born, at some time and to someone who loved them. She couldn't bear to think anything else.

67

As she drifted away on a tide of painkiller, she felt again the touch of a small warm hand against her own.

CHAPTER NINE

A MEETING ON THE WAY

Cornelia found herself thinking about that dream as the days went past. It saddened her, and yet she could not feel guilty. The road she had taken was not an easy one. She had given that journey everything she had.

Was there something missing in her character? Some vital sensitivity that made her fail to feel conscience-ridden as someone else might have?

She said nothing to Amanda, though she knew her companion suspected that something was on her mind. They'd been together too long, knew each other too well. But Amanda never intruded until she was ready to talk, and that was a comfort.

Lucius came to visit, interrupting her examination of her conscience. Amanda seemed particularly glad to see him, for she knew the business he brought would pull her charge out of whatever problem haunted her.

What he brought was a contract for the book.

"Lucius!" Cornelia exclaimed. "Did you tell them that I probably won't live to finish this? I have about a hundred and fifty hand-written pages, which count less than typed ones. I may do another hundred, and then I may not live to do another one. This offer is too huge—I can't accept money for something I can't guarantee."

The muggy heat of the East Texas fall was bothering the lawyer. He had removed his spring-weight jacket, and the fan was turned up, but he still perspired.

He mopped his forehead, which went, these days, a lot farther back than it used to. "Cornelia, what you don't realize is that this will sell, finished or not.

"Adamson says that if you...have to stop...he will write a note at that point. The edition will have photos of every step of your career.

"Your finest parts, your own ballets, the stills from the movies—it will be full of pictures! Handsomely bound, too."

"But what do I need money for? I have enough to see me through, and my niece will have more than she needs, after I go."

He smiled, his expression smug. "I have a plan. You have worried for years about dancers who get too old or too ill to continue their careers. Why not establish a major trust that will help them? Maybe establish a home for them, where they can sit and talk and reminisce and lie to their hearts' content?"

She felt excitement building inside her. She breathed deeply—no need to get the heart so upset that it kicked off too soon. Blood warmed her face, and she felt herself tingling with enthusiasm.

"Yes! I have always wanted something like that, but the time passed and I didn't do it. Set it up. Have the Company oversee the running of it, if they're willing. A trustee if they're not. It should be good publicity for them, if nothing else.

"A quarter of a million dollars, invested well, should take care of a number of people, just with the interest. Maybe others will add to the fund. I'd love to see that happen, Lucius."

"I thought you would. Adamson says for you not to feel burdened. Write if you feel like it; quit when you don't. What you have is fine. Write anecdotes and don't bother trying to fit them together. That will be taken care of, later." Lucius's lips tightened.

She took his hand. He had been a good friend for so many years, and now he was making her feel that even this final indignity might serve a good purpose.

"Get Amanda to help run it," she said softly, glancing toward the connecting door. "She will be lonely. This will give her something to do that she'll love."

Amanda interrupted her, coming in with tea. But Lucius nodded, and Cornelia knew he would keep her companion too busy to grieve.

He stayed a week. They planned the foundation, the home, and they also went over her completed pages. He liked the contents, though she saw him concealing his amusement at her spelling.

"Get someone to proof this before you send it to the typist," she begged. "I was good at everything in school except spelling."

"You have enough emotion and interest here to make up for any amount of bad spelling," he said. "It's fine work. You make the people you have known come to life on the pages, and that isn't easy.

"You've put yourself here, too. Readers are going to feel they knew you. Let me take this with me, will you?" He looked anxious, and she nodded.

"Things can become confused, when someone dies," she said. "I know that Cynthia and Coral and my aunt are going to descend on the house like a couple of buzzards, grabbing for anything they can get. I've seen things like that happen.

"Amanda is going to lock everything away, once I'm gone. Even before she calls the doctor or the undertaker."

Lucius looked shocked. "Surely not!"

"For you or for me it wouldn't work that way. But I wasn't too young to understand what happened when Mom's aunt died. Relatives descended on the house like a bunch of locusts, carrying things out before the funeral."

She remembered the appalled whispers she had overheard among the adults in the family. "Uncle Ira's daughter had to call the sheriff and get him to make them unload so the poor old man would have a chair to sit in or a bed for the night."

"I cannot imagine anyone so callous," Lucius said. "Surely your own people wouldn't...."

"Once burned, twice shy," she said. "It's just as well to send off the manuscript I have completed with you. Anything else I complete, I'll have Amanda mail as I get enough together. I can just see Emily or Coral burning my work without reading it, they'd be so fearful that I was giving away family secrets or telling about my disgraceful past."

He agreed, and when he left the pages were in a neat bundle under his arm. Cornelia found it hard to say goodbye, for she knew it was for the last time.

She managed to control herself until he was gone, and the sound of the station wagon was lost among the trees. "Amanda, I'm getting soft. I want to cry," she said. The old woman sat on the edge of her bed and caught her into her arms. "You just go ahead."

Her bosom might be bony, but the heart beneath it was loving, and Cornelia eased her grief. One friend, at least, was with her to the end.

The countersigned contract came back with a notation that the advance would be placed in trust at once, when it was received. With that, Cornelia turned her attention to writing the book. She had not reckoned with the newspapers.

DYING DANCER SIGNS
QUARTER-MILLION CONTRACT

a headline screamed, and Eric read it to her over the phone on the morning it appeared. He came out with a copy of the paper, and they worried together about the effect the publicity would have on her relatives.

"Coral will have conniptions," Eric said.

"What about Emily?" Cornelia groaned. "I'm going to have family coming out my ears, now. People will beg for money that I have already given away. Blast and damn those reporters!"

"I'm going to hire watchmen," Eric said. "Where there is money concerned, away off down here, you can never guess what people may do. There are some nasty weirdoes in the world."

Cornelia was startled. It seemed enough that she was dying. The thought of being held hostage or something of the sort was appalling.

"Worse things happen every day," he sighed. "A couple of years ago some doped-up kids beat the Carters to hamburger with bicycle chains. They live over on the other side of Chalmers, down in the river bottoms. They had no money, but somebody just wanted to kill a couple of old people for kicks."

She shivered, and Eric touched her shoulder. "I'll get in touch with the security people. They're a good bunch, and it won't hurt to have somebody on guard at night. You'll never know they're here. Not unless you need them."

"Thanks, Bro," she said. "It's good to be home again, Eric. I missed you a lot. Nobody else reads my mind."

"Not many read ancient Greek, these days," he said, his face perfectly deadpan.

They laughed together, and after he left Cornelia sat staring at the painting now on the wall. A path angled up a mountain, with rough boulders heaped on either side. A tuft of green thrust defiantly into the warm light from a setting sun.

Tall peaks loomed to the left of the composition, but the path itself was lost in a maze of stony rubble on a slope. The ramparts of the mountains had been scoured by weather to the shade of antique pewter, and the light echoed among the stones.

She blinked and turned to the door, where Ella brought in her supper. Outside, the forest beyond the lawn outside was gold on green. She had almost wandered into another painting.

Later, she wrote for a couple of hours. When Amanda insisted that she rest, she had several pages ready to go off.

She welcomed a warm shower, feeling tension leave her weary muscles. She stepped out into a downy towel Amanda held...and into a storm of emotional upheaval.

Coral's voice came through the door. "You come right out here, Cornelia. I want to talk to you."

"Oh, Lord!" she sighed. "I am so tired, Amanda. How can I bear it?"

"I will go and throw her into the front yard," Amanda said, very clearly and distinctly.

Cornelia shook her head. "No. I'd like for you to, and it's what she deserves, but it would be awful if everyone got what he deserved, now wouldn't it? I'll go, but stay close. I may take you up on your offer, yet."

"Cornelia Watson, I do not understand you! I never have. Of all the irresponsible things to do, giving away hundreds of thousands of dollars to a bunch of strangers, away from your own flesh and blood! But you never think of anyone but yourself.

"You want headlines. Big Name Watson! Old dancers, indeed! When you have family!" Coral was getting impatient.

Amanda helped her into the freshly made bed and pulled the sheet up. Glaring at Coral, she left the room, but Cornelia knew she kept a close eye on this encounter.

Chapter Ten

Trailing Tears

Coral's sweetness-and-light act had disappeared completely. She ignored Amanda, storming to the foot of Cornelia's bed and glaring at her until her sister thought she was uglier than the gargoyle topping the tall head-board.

"I take it that you do not approve of my plans for my advance on the book?" she asked. Her hands were laced tightly in her lap to keep them from following their strong impulse to throw something at Coral.

"You would do something like that! Instead of doing things for your own flesh and blood, you set up some stupid trust for people who've never done anything more useful than tippy-toeing around on a stage!"

Coral's face once more matched her name. Had Mom somehow intuited what sort of child her second daughter would become?

"The last time you were here, I offered to write you a check for any reasonable amount. You said you needed nothing. I took you at your word. Why should I consult you—or anyone else—about disposing of money I earn?"

"It's family money! We deserve our share!"

Cornelia felt herself growing warm. She pulled at the lace collar of her nightgown and fanned the sheet to make a breeze. Before opening her mouth, she got a grip on herself, and her years of harsh discipline helped.

Still, she knew her tone was angrier than she had intended. "What has the family done to earn one thin dime? Not you or Cynthia or Emily has ever so much as attended a

performance of my work, though Eric came to all he could
manage to. I sent tickets and air fare, but you could not bear
to find yourselves mistaken about me.

"Did you volunteer to type my manuscripts? Did you offer to help me organize my notes? You earned nothing."

Coral dropped into the rocker. "Of course we didn't
want to see you make a fool of yourself. Cornelia, an East
Texas farm girl does not become a dancer—you couldn't be
anything but ridiculous.

"You had to be sleeping with somebody rich and important to make all that money and to get into the movies. We
know how that works. We didn't want to be embarrassed."

Cornelia closed her eyes and breathed as deeply as possible. When she opened them again, Coral was watching her,
an alarmed expression dawning on her face. But Cornelia got
herself in hand.

"And how do you rationalize to yourself any rights to
the advance money?"

"It isn't so much the money, it's the book. We know
you're telling all sorts of scandalous things. People will
know the sort of life you've lived, and Emily and I can't
stand the thought of dragging the family that low.

"The money won't begin to pay us for what we'll face
when the book comes out and people start snickering behind
our backs."

"Oh, my God!"

"There you go, taking the Lord's name in vain. The
book is probably full of filth."

"Amanda!" Cornelia called, "Will you show this bitch
out of my house?"

Amanda appeared with the promptness of a genie pop-
ping from a bottle. "I will. Come with me—or would you
prefer being dragged?"

Coral rose, her face scarlet. "I'll go. But if you think this
is the end, you wait. That's the reason Emily burned all
Mom's...." The red leached from her cheeks, leaving them
deathly pale.

"Burned Mom's what?" Cornelia leaned forward and
gripped her sister's wrist with one swollen hand. "Tell me, or
I will put Eric onto you. He can find out anything."

Coral seemed to shrink. "Mom's books and stories that she wrote. Emily didn't want her sister's memory to be shamed by the stuff she was writing when she died."

Cornelia sank back, gasping. She clearly remembered finding her mother often, bent over her desk in the evenings, writing away either in her journal or onto a lined pad. She had never thought to wonder what the latter might be.

After a moment she was able to speak. "I am older than you and was at home after Mom died. When did this happen, and how did Dad allow it?"

Coral looked as if she might faint. "It happened after you left. Aunt Emily didn't know about the manuscripts, before that. The older ones were in Mom's big trunk in the attic. The rest were in her writing desk, in the bottom drawer, covered with bills and papers.

"It was years before Emily got around to clearing it all out. She was shocked when she realized...."

"What?"

"That Mom never stopped wanting to be a dancer. That just about killed Emily; two in her own family!"

Cornelia felt a stab of pain and held her breath until it subsided. "Mom's journals—did she burn them, too?"

"No." The word was barely audible. "She couldn't find them, and Dad wouldn't let her go searching for them. He was...he was very angry about those manuscripts.

"He kept saying that Emily killed Mom twice, and I never understood what he meant. But Emily says he always allowed Mom to have her way more than was decent."

Cornelia stared at her sister. Breath burned in her chest, and her temples drummed. She felt a vicious desire to attack that silly woman standing beside the bed, her arm still gripped by Amanda's thin hand. But she fought down her anger, smoothed her breathing, quieted her surging blood.

"And why have you always accepted Emily's word as Revealed Truth?" she asked. "What did she ever do that was useful or honorable or even halfway kind?

"She has been a parasite all her life. She never accomplished anything, only criticized those who got out and did things.

"How did she persuade you that I, who never knowingly did anything dishonorable, could possibly be the sort she claims I am?"

The thought of her mother's work, representing as it must have done hard-won bits of time scavenged from house and farm work, filled her with wild grief and loss. She couldn't bear to look at Coral.

"I want you to go. I will not see you again, and I prefer that you and Emily do not come to my funeral. Tell Emily that if I were the cursing kind, she would have mine." She closed her eyes and listened as Amanda led the subdued woman from the room.

When her steps returned, Cornelia looked up at her. "I want to find those journals. I need to know my mother, before it's too late.

"She died at a time when I needed her badly, but I was busy and I put it behind me. Now I need to know. Could you look, for the sake of my peace of mind?"

"Glad to," said Amanda. "But this is a big house, and I don't know all the cubbies. You ought to—any kid raised in this kind of house usually knows all the hidey-holes."

Cornelia frowned. She knew the place from attic to fruit cellar. She had her own private nooks, too. "Behind the loose plank in the attic might be a good spot to begin the search."

But that was empty. Amanda searched from top to bottom of the old house, guided by Cornelia when she ran out of ideas. Night found her tired and cobwebby, but with no journals in hand.

Cornelia went to bed trying to think of someplace that would be large enough to hold the fat leather books, yet secret enough not to have been located by Emily, once her father died. She woke, and her eyes focused on the tall mahogany dresser that matched her bed.

There were candle sconces on either side, above small handkerchief drawers. There were those four small drawers, two big deep ones and what Mom called the slipper drawer, concealed behind what seemed to be a carved finishing piece along its bottom!

She looked at the clock. Five...too early to call Amanda, but she was almost certain she had found the place where the missing books were hidden.

This had been Mom and Dad's room. Emily could not have rummaged here as long as Dad lived, and once he was gone she might never have suspected the existence of that concealed drawer. Her and Mom's family had not run to heavy Victorian furniture.

Cornelia swung her feet over the edge of the bed and clung to the headboard for a moment until the dizziness subsided. Her walker was at hand; she stumbled to the dresser and, groaning softly, sank to her waterlogged knees.

The slipper drawer was quite invisible, but she remembered how to slip her fingers along the bottom, to find the two notches. She tugged, but the drawer stuck. It must have been years since it was opened.

A sound at the door made her turn, to find Amanda staring at her. "What in the name of Goshen are you doing?"

"I found the journals, I'm sure. Help me, Amanda. I can't get the thing open!" She was almost crying with weariness and pain.

Her companion helped her up and swept her back into bed. "You stay still while I open this up. Could have called, but no, had to do it yourself. Just like you—pig-headed!"

Cornelia smiled at Amanda's back, bent over the stubborn drawer. "Maybe, but I found it. I remembered that was the place Mom sometimes let me hide things from Coral when she was tiny. Emily would never find it, and the journals just have to be there."

"Here she comes!" There was a soft groaning of wood on wood, and the drawer slid out. Cornelia could smell old paper and mildewed leather and stale air.

"Six little red leather books are in here." Amanda beamed as she lifted them from their hiding place. "Look here! Seems to be a jewel box! Look at this, Cornelia."

She reached for the musty box, but she felt she already knew its contents. "The treasures. I wondered what happened to them, after she died, but I was so busy resisting Emily's bossing that I hadn't time to search."

A ROAD OF STARS, BY ARDATH MAYHAR

The blue velvet was fragile with age, its yellow silk lining split. But the contents were there: Mom's pin, gold, rimmed with seed pearls and centered with a chip diamond. Grandpa's round gold watch with engraved swirls of ferns and flowers.

Cornelia wound it, and the ponderous ticking filled her with wonder and nostalgia. She pulled another, smaller pin on its side, and fairy chimes rang a short melody.

Tears filled her eyes as she looked into the box again. There were her baby things. A silver bracelet, too large for a ring but just right for a baby's fat wrist. Two tiny rings, one gold, one silver, and a locket. Gramma's bracelet with Mom's teething marks imprinted into the soft rose gold.

There was the necklace made of yellow stones, set in steel, strangely beautiful because she just recalled Gramma wearing it. Cornelia held up a string of cut quartz crystals, and beneath it was the string of hand-made pottery beads.

She laid the things again in the box and handed it to Amanda. "Put it into one of the handkerchief drawers, will you? I want to be able to look at them. But now I want the journals."

Sending Amanda to eat her breakfast at last, Cornelia leafed through the most faded of the red books. The date inside its cover was June 3, 1931. Mom had been twelve or thirteen.

The paper had yellowed, but the pages turned easily and without cracking. She came to the first entry, where a spray of roses was sketched in gray across the page. The handwriting was upright, angular, her mother's distinctive hand.

"I am desperately unhappy," were the first words she read. This had, after all, been a very young girl, apt to take trivial things too seriously. But the next words struck her to the heart.

"Emily has persuaded Mama and Papa that they must refuse to let me dance."

And how well she knew the agony of that!

80

CHAPTER ELEVEN

ERIC

She found that, even with the books in hand, she couldn't read farther. Some inner fear made her open and close them, one after another, only scanning a random line from time to time. She needed reinforcement of some sort before she could venture into her mother's private world.

She ate her breakfast absent-mindedly. When she was again in the reclining chair beside her bed, she fingered the books, knowing that the mother she recalled was about to be changed, perhaps beyond recognition, by the things she wrote into these journals. It was a frightening thought. Amanda held her peace, although she would have been justified in grumbling, after so much effort, to find Cornelia reluctant to read the hard-won volumes. She quietly went away with Ella to the kitchen, leaving her charge to come to grips with the problem.

Cornelia, once reminded of their existence, found that she remembered those fat red books very well. Mom at the desk, bills and ledgers for the farm bookkeeping strewn around her, had often taken one of the red books from the drawer and written in it.

She had resented the time Mom spent writing and keeping the farm books. Perhaps that was why she had not recalled the existence of the journals until reminded by Coral's reference to manuscripts.

She smiled sadly. It had never occurred to her that beneath her mother's shining chestnut hair had been a quick brain, knowing its own identity and its own goals. Probably, on some deep level, that mind had wrestled with its own frustrations.

She examined the book in her lap. This oldest volume was faded along the spine and at the corners. The edges were scuffed, and she suspected that it had ridden along in pockets and bicycle baskets. There was a stain on the end page that looked suspiciously like Coke. Another was a grass stain.

She could almost see the small girl who had written these angular lines, as she turned the pages. On the flyleaf was a tiny sketch, a dancer soaring into a leap, arms floating, toes pointed, the ankle of the trailing leg curved precisely upward in perfect position. All the instincts had been there: Mom's eye had caught what her body had not had the chance to learn.

She read that first line again. Now that she was under control, it didn't hurt her so much to think of her mother's frustration.

She had been a happy, outgoing woman, as far as Cornelia could remember. The loss of her dream hadn't been allowed to sour her disposition or make her resentful of those who did the things she longed for. Surely she could be as strong as her mother had been!

But not right now. She had to rest, for she had lost ground in the past weeks. Her hands seemed too heavy for her wrists, her arms hanging like lead weights from her weary shoulders. Breathing exhausted her.

"Amanda!" she called. She touched the small bell on the bedside table. "I must go back to bed!"

There was no reply. She and Ella must have closed the door to keep the steams from their tomato canning from permeating the house.

But there came a step in the hall. "Need something? Let me help," said Eric.

Cornelia felt tears of relief start into her eyes. She was learning to despise the dependency her illness caused, but she seemed not to mind Eric's help.

"I am so glad to see you," she gasped, as he lifted her into the bed and spread the sheet over her legs. "I was going to call you, when I felt better, but here you are, like magic."

He sat in the rocker and stretched out his long legs. "I'm taking advantage of your invitation."

"Invitation?" For a moment she couldn't imagine what he meant.

"To refugee out here, when Cyn gets on a high horse. She and Coral and Emily have joined forces and are turning the air blue with weepings and wailings and gnashings of teeth.

"I can't talk sense to them, and they have Rafe Pierce, their preacher, stirred up to the point at which he intends to come out here and bullyrag you back into Christian behavior."

"I'll attend to that when the time comes," Cornelia said. "There's something else. But first I need the medicine—one of the tablets in the box there."

He poured water from the Thermos pitcher and offered her the tablet; five seconds after she swallowed it the thudding of her heart eased, and she felt a blessed remoteness stealing over her.

"About Mom's journals?" he asked. "Amanda told me you found them."

She nodded, feeling as if she were floating over the bed instead of lying on it. "Not only that. About Mom. Do you remember—you're older and you might—if she seemed happy? All those years of farming and raising kids, could you tell if she seemed satisfied?"

His pale eyes went remote, as they did when he looked inside himself. His expression was still and withdrawn, as he searched his memory. He was thinking with all his might, as he (and she) tended to do everything.

Then he smiled, the wrinkles about his gray eyes deepening, his lips curving in that joyful arc that recalled to her the boy he had been. "Yes. I can truthfully say she was one of the happiest people I have ever known."

Cornelia sighed with relief. "You're not just trying to make me feel better?"

"No. It's true. Neely, just because a person doesn't get one thing he wants from life, it doesn't mean that everything is spoiled for him or her.

"Think about yourself. There are many elements you didn't have, because there wasn't the time and you had no energy for anything except dancing. Did the lack of those other things ruin your life?"

"Of course not! You're quite right. Probably it's being sick that makes me worry so. Tell me all you can remember about our mother, will you?"

He began talking, very quietly, his voice as soothing as the hum of the bees outside in the morning glory vine climbing the ash tree. "She was the brightest person, and not just mentally. She—I guess you could say she glowed. Her hair was shiny, and her eyes, and her smile.

"My first memory of her is back when I still slept in a crib. I must have been about two. She was bending over me, reaching down, and something shiny swung from her neck. She was laughing and talking to me, and I still remember the way she smelled, like soap and clean wind and new leaves.

"When she knew you were on the way, even I, who was only three, was pleased because she was so happy. We all went around beaming, and Dad whistled as he followed the mules up and down the rows with me holding onto his hip pocket and taking every step with him, collecting fish worms as the dirt turned."

"You weren't jealous?"

He snorted. "I was crazy with joy. By the time you came, I was nearly four, and I needed somebody to play with. We were too far from neighbors for playmates, and I thought you were going to rise from your crib and play a game of catch with me in about six weeks.

"By the time I knew better, you had me hooked. Mom let me help tend to you, right along with her. She trusted me, and she trusted you, too, when the time came. She trusted everyone...too much, in some cases."

"Emily...," said Cornelia.

"Not just Emily. There were people in the church who squabbled and told lies about each other. It took Mom years to get fed up with it and stop going. They kept her upset until she gave up on them.

"Once she got rid of the dogmas, she knew that it had been a poor excuse for searching for the truth, anyway. We were lucky, you know.

"I know people raised in churches who are superstitious as a bunch of savages, afraid of their own imaginations and fully expecting God to play nasty tricks on them if they don't hew to the line. We didn't have to overcome that sort of thing."

"Coral mentioned to me once that Mom's being an agnostic is probably the reason why I am such a sinner," Cornelia said, her tone dry.

Eric laughed. "Agnostic? I don't know. She loved everything and was kind to the deserving and the undeserving alike. But she hadn't one minute of patience for a phony or a liar, and that was her problem with the church, I suspect.

"Cyn gets put out with me for the same thing. I'm too much like Mom to suit her."

"That's what I needed to know," Cornelia said. "I needed to know that the happy woman I remember wasn't something I made up."

Eric stretched his legs even farther, tilting the rocker perilously. He frowned. "She told me something, once, that I've never forgotten. She said that you do your best with what you have and don't fret after the things you are denied. The most miserable people she knew had a lot that should make them happy, but they never seemed to notice it because they were so busy running after what they couldn't get."

"That sounds like her. She focused herself on what she was doing, all the way. I always felt special, because of that, and I suspect you did, too."

"I wonder if her death cut Coral off before she could get her feet on the ground?" Eric asked.

"Probably." Cornelia shifted her swollen body between the sheets. "And Dad? How was he, after I left? Did he ever regret going on with the farm, instead of taking up something else?"

"Dad wasn't well. I didn't know it for years, but he had a heart condition long before it made itself really bothersome. That's why Emily got away with bullying him; he just hadn't the strength to stand up to her.

"Once you left, he felt terrible to know that you had really gone, and he hadn't ignored her enough to give you enough money to last until you got settled. It made him sicker." He gave a harsh grunt.

"And that, of course, gave Emily more of a handle on him."

"He seemed lost at Mom's funeral," Cornelia said. "That must have been why he let Emily come to keep house for him. What a terrible mistake!"

Eric reached to take her hand. "Don't make the error of seeing Emily as a monster, Neely. She has always been miserable and useless, but it isn't altogether her own fault. She didn't set out to make a career of Cornelia-bashing. She was taught to be that way.

"Mom was, too, of course, but she had too much common sense. She examined the things her people drummed into her, I figure, someplace along the way and threw out the whole lot, once she learned better."

Cornelia stared at him. Had she been unthinkingly hostile in the same way Emily and Coral had been? Even as a reaction to their attitude, that would be irrational, and she had prided herself on rationality, if little else. Emotion had not consciously directed her decisions, no matter what her feelings might demand.

She laughed. "So here I am, old enough to die, quite literally, and still behaving like an over-aged and oversized child. Should I apologize to them?" She meant it.

"Oh, God, no!" Eric straightened and grabbed her hand. "Believe me, it wouldn't make them a bit different at this point, and it would bring them down around your ears.

"No, just understand what the problem is and try not to let it influence you from here on in. They don't really intend to behave like...mental incompetents." He took a deep breath.

"They think they're anxious about your 'spiritual welfare,' not your money. Without the money, you could go your merry way without a word from them, but they don't know it. And nobody is as impervious to reason as somebody who thinks she is saving your soul."

Now she laughed in earnest, though it set off a coughing fit. Eric was a dear, honest and patient. He was beset with recalcitrant womenfolk, but he seemed to deal with it well.

Amanda put her head into the door. "Lunch is ready, for a wonder. We put up fifty quarts of tomatoes this morning. Makes me feel like a Pioneer Woman. You ought to buy me a sunbonnet and a hoe!"

Now Cornelia choked on her laughter, for the thought of Amanda in a be-ruffled sunbonnet, designed to keep women-folk subdued with heat stroke, was something she could not envision.

"You sound better," Amanda said. "I thought having your brother here would cheer you up. Now you come eat with us in your chair. If you can laugh like that, you can make it."

Eric lifted her into the chair, and she rode triumphantly to the kitchen, where the long table beneath the ceiling fan was set for four. Amanda added a plate and pushed her chair close, as Ella set a tureen of stew beside the plates of sliced tomatoes and cucumbers and the pile of corn on the cob.

She ate, strangely enough, with some appetite. But somehow she knew that she would not make this short journey to the kitchen very many times more.

CHAPTER TWELVE

FROM THE JOURNALS

With Eric's support, Cornelia began reading the leather books. Over her protests, her brother pushed her chair onto the front porch in the cool of the next morning, placed a table at her elbow, and pulled up a rocker beyond it.

"When we get tired, we can listen to the birds or watch the kittens," he insisted, and she found the rustle of the rose vines, the scampering of the kittens, and the encouragement of a mockingbird stimulating.

She began reading aloud, selectively, for many entries were dry information about the Oklahoma farm, on which their mother had worked from the time she was a small child until their move to Texas, where they opened a general merchandise store.

As soon as her family moved to East Texas the entries grew more interesting.

"Here's a mention of Dad," Cornelia said. "Barry Watson came into the store today, making eyes at me. I like him, but he can be so silly. I told him, right out, if he wants to talk to me he'd better do it in words, because I don't understand monkey-faces.

"He turned red as Mom's apron and left. I hope I didn't hurt his feelings."

Eric chuckled. "I don't envy him, courting Mom. She wasn't susceptible to normal courting procedures, and the wonder is that any of us ever made it into the world.

"You're a lot like her, Neely. She thought things that most people consider to be important the worst kind of nonsense."

"Like making eyes at girls?"

"Exactly. Listen. Here's something from the book she wrote in the first five years of her marriage." He squinted at the page.

"It's funny how you think, as a child, that your life will go just as you planned it. I wanted so badly to dance, but now I see that by the time I realized what I wanted to do, I was too old to begin serious training. Besides, I would never have given up Barry and living on the farm. Still, I need something more that is my own. I have sent away for some books on writing. If I can't dance, I'll tell stories, though if Emily dreamed I intended such a thing she would have hysterics.

"Poor Emily. She has no backbone and less ambition. Since Morton died almost at the altar, she has been so pitiful—I must be kinder to her."

Cornelia was silent, thinking. That was why she had been given lessons from the time she was four. It was why Mom had connived and managed to find money enough for Marisa. Somehow, she knew her daughter had inherited her need to dance.

"Do you remember how Mom told about her Gramma dancing all over the Methodist Church when she got the spirit?" she asked. "She must have had a desperate need for it to do that, for Methodists of her time thought it was worse than sinful. While others were speaking in tongues, she danced."

Cornelia's gaze followed the mother of the kittens, who dashed across the yard, hotly pursued by a mockingbird. But she was thinking of generations of frustrated women, solidly persuaded that it was the Devil who made them want to dance.

"So for years, Mom wrote stories, instead. Or books. Nobody knows." Eric turned another page. "I wonder! Knowing Mom, I'd say she marketed what she wrote. That doesn't mean she would do it under her own name, necessarily, with Emily in the family. Do you suppose that was how she got the money for my dancing classes?"

Eric's eyes widened. Then they narrowed. "Wouldn't Emily be staggered if her bonfire just burned manuscripts that had already been published?" His curving grin flickered for a moment.

Cornelia nodded. "She would have used a pseudonym. Somebody would have known, otherwise. Someplace in the journals, there has to be a clue. And there are all those magazines—the ones she saved and had bound into volumes. I wondered why she did that, but I'll bet that at least some have her stories in them.

"And all of her books! She had so many that ones she wrote under a pseudonym would never be noticed. I think we're onto something!" She felt more alive than she had in a long while.

Eric grinned, his face alight with enthusiasm. He began turning pages, skimming their contents, and she did the same.

After an hour of that, she had to go back to bed, but Eric persisted through the afternoon, stopping for a snack at supper time and diving back into the journals again. She went to bed knowing that he was on the job.

"I have danced a matinee and evening performance, gone to a reception and stayed up until the wee hours without being as tired as I get just sitting in my chair," she told Amanda, as her companion made the room ready for the night. "It isn't easy, Amanda."

"I know." Her hands were gentle as they smoothed the light coverlet. She turned the fan low, and the fragrance of leaves and blossoming shrubs came through the window to cool Cornelia's swollen face.

"Now take your medicine and go to sleep. I'd bet your brother comes up with your answer before day. He has forgotten it's night, and he's in the living groom reading away."

Cornelia floated away on a cloud of synthetic sleep. She woke suddenly when the mockingbird stopped singing, very late. Only tree frogs and crickets were keeping up the night-noises. She could see a patch of stars through a gap in the branches of the ash tree.

"Neely?" came a whisper.

"I'm awake. Come in!"

She touched the switch, and the bedside lamp bloomed into light. Eric stood in the door, grinning like a fiend.

"Found it! Just where we thought it would be! She wrote it into the book with an eye to Emily's finding it, some day. She pretended this was an author she admired and named the magazine, with the month. Here, let me read it to you." He pulled the rocker to the light.

"Yesterday I read a story that I thought was most interesting. A new writer, Lillian Carlyle, is the author, and the magazine expects more of her work in the future. Emily would not approve of her story, as she doesn't so much as mention religion in all her three thousand words, but she tells a better tale because of that. I am saving the August issue of the *Scriveners*, in which the story appeared. I believe that I will save my magazines, from now on, and have them bound for future reference."

He looked up. "All the clues are there. Emily's disapproval, the magazine title, the month, even. Hidden to someone like Emily, who has no imagination, but obvious to someone really looking."

Cornelia held out a hand, and he pulled her higher on her pillows. "We can search the bound copies tomorrow. She had to sell stories! The farm never could have made enough extra for my schooling, and even with the scholarship there were a lot of expenses.

"That's why Dad couldn't help me, once Mom died. That source of money came to an end." She stared up at Eric. "Do you suppose he knew?"

"Of course. They never kept things from each other. What came up usually came out, too, as Emily knew too well. She would never have suspected Mom of having a real secret."

Numbering the words in the story was the main clue. Anybody bright enough to catch that, along with the reference to Emily, would probably know that Lillian Carlyle was Mom, if they had an inkling at all about her writing.

Eric kissed her forehead. "You go back to sleep. Not a peep until morning! We'll spend the day looking." He snapped out the light and was gone.

Cornelia slept deeply, and only when the mockingbird tuned up again at dawn did she open her eyes and smile at the gargoyle face on the headboard. "Good morning, you ugly cuss," she said.

However, when Amanda came to help her wash and dress, she found that she had no strength. The excitement had been too much, and she had to fidget over her breakfast while Eric ate.

When he came to the door, she said, "Bring them in here. Please! I can help look, and if I get tired I can watch you looking. I can't bear not to be in on this."

He brought an armful at a time and piled them onto a card table Ella brought. Cornelia picked up a bound volume and found it to be for the last six months of 1943— *Cosmopolitan Magazine*.

She smiled at the ads, which she remembered from her childhood: Gap-o-sis, Pepsodent, and Ipana. She took the time to browse a bit before she began turning to the tables of contents.

The byline she wanted was not in the first, the second, or the third magazine in the volume. October's issue had stories by Paul Gallico and a couple of others who had become household names.

Six stories, a full-length novel, and articles dealing, first-hand, with the wars in Europe and Asia. Current magazines didn't hold a candle to these oldies.

On the contents page of the November issue was the listing, "Another Time, Another Place," by Lillian Carlyle.

"Eric!"

He glanced up, as if his mind still wandered among the stories and articles in the collection he held. His eyes lit up. "Found it?"

"Here." She handed him the book, and he read the first paragraph and chuckled.

"The heroine's name is Cornelia. This was published the year you were born. And the hero's name is Barry. Now tell me that is a coincidence."

"This is like finding someone we never knew existed," she said. "Eric, this was our Mom, who milked the cows and built fence and sat up with us when we were sick. And we never knew her. She did find something all her own, and it makes me feel better to know that."

He rose and bent over her. "Now we know for certain. We can take as long as we need to work through the shelves of volumes, but you need to rest right now. Amanda will skin me, if I let you get too tired.

"I'll go through the bookshelves to see if we have the novels, too. Lie back when I take this pillow out. Now... okay? You rest. Sleep if you can, and I'll keep looking."

She lay thinking of this new mother she had found. Denied one road, Mom had explored another. She'd trudged away down it, undeterred by the fact that it had to be hard for an East Texas farm wife in the Forties to sell her work to big Eastern publishers.

She wondered what her own road would have been, if Mom had not managed to make the money for her training. Would she have married Charlie and mothered those children?

Or would there have been other possibilities? She stared at the painting Amanda had hung on the wall that morning.

A street in a small town held big trees, leaning over the pavement and casting blue shadows on the pale cement. Old-fashioned homes were set back from the sidewalks, their wide lawns studded with rosebushes and hollies and dogwoods.

An overcast morning held silver-blue mist, rising in the distance. The sun was silver-gold beyond the branches of the second oak on the left. What if she had taken a road like that?

Chapter Thirteen

The Only Road

Cornelia had been dreading a visit from Emily's preacher. Mr. Pierce was probably the fire-eating variety of Methodist minister sometimes still cropping up in the Bible Belt, and to explain to such a person her personal beliefs would be undignified, if not impossible. It made her angry to be forced to defend herself in such a way.

Besides, she resented being deflected from her researches into her mother's published work. So far, she and Eric had located a dozen stories, a novelette, and two articles in the magazines they had searched, besides seven novels, two of them literary, the others romantic.

When Amanda told her the preacher had arrived, she was glad Eric was still staying with her. He could come to her rescue, if needed.

It was early afternoon, and, being July, it was hot. But the year had been a mild one, for East Texas, and the shade of the trees, the ceiling fans, and the high-ceiled house itself kept the temperature fairly pleasant.

The window was open, as Cornelia liked it, and an orchard oriole was singing as the minister entered her room.

The man's near-sighted eyes were pale and defenseless in his mild face. She was sorry for him, for her kin had evidently filled him with the most pernicious nonsense.

He was obviously terrified of the sort of Jezebel he must haul back into the fold. If she had been a true Jezebel, she thought with amusement, she could have eaten him alive and spat out his bones.

But he seemed to be braver than he looked. His hand came out to meet hers, as he said, "Raiford Pierce, Ma'am. Your sister and your aunt are old friends of mine, as well as faithful churchgoers."

She smiled, relaxing. He would probably be horrified at her unorthodoxy, but this was a man who would listen. He cared about people, it was perfectly plain to her, and that was the key.

"Thank you for visiting me, Mr. Pierce, although I am afraid you have troubled yourself unnecessarily. My sister and my aunt have never bothered to learn the truth about me or about my career. They waste a lot of worry." She hoped that was mild enough. It was accurate, in an understated sort of way.

His pale blue eyes lighted up with relief. "That is a great satisfaction. Which church holds your membership?"

Later, she congratulated herself on the tactful manner in which she had explained to him something of her unusual beliefs, without seeming to attack his entirely orthodox and uninspired dogmas.

The hardest thing had been making him understand what it was that she had done with her life.

"Didn't they tell you that I was a dancer?" she asked him, at one point. "I would still be dancing a bit, choreographing a great deal, and teaching as well, if it had not been for my illness."

"They told me you—danced." His tone was slightly questioning. She could imagine their actual words.

"I danced. I was not a prostitute. One does not achieve what I did by wasting her powers on sex and manipulation."

Her words seemed to shock him, but she had gone on, "I could go to any country and dance with any troupe in the world, and the theaters would be full.

"Being forcibly retired from all that, I believe that it will not be too arrogant to say that without sounding egotistical. My brother can show you the press clippings.

"I have traveled in almost every nation of the world. Prime Ministers and Party Chairmen, educators and academics and critics have been my friends. My work was appreciated widely."

He looked dazed. "I understood from your aunt that your career had been quite different. Does she know the truth of this?"

Cornelia sighed at that point. "If you can persuade her to listen, you are a better man than I. She has closed her ears to all explanation and to all proof. Rationality is not one of my aunt's strong points."

She had slipped past his attempts to make her beliefs jibe with his orthodoxy, for he was a good little man with little imagination. "I have spent my life in a search for truth," she said.

"Although it is not the truth you think of as the only one, it is a valid one. Many wise people have understood the things I have put into dance, and many caring people have told me they are the better for seeing my work. That, to me, seems the most important thing of all.

"If my only concern were that of saving my own soul from some hypothetical damnation, then I would be a monster of self-centered arrogance. I am not the best person I could possibly be, I am certain. But I am far from being the person my kin have told you that I am." She hoped that got through to him.

At last he desisted, unsatisfied that she was what he called "Right with God," yet understanding that she was quite ready to die in her present situation.

Amanda came to remind her of her medicine, and Pierce rose to leave. He had been shocked to find that the worshipful attitudes of the women in his church were not shared by all females.

She had asked him hard questions, and she had replied to his with hard answers. She could see astonishment in his eyes as he said, "I will pray for you."

"A sincere prayer by a good person never is wasted," she said. "I will appreciate that. I prayed as I danced, giving every moment of pain, of wrenching effort as my gift to the Maker of Universes. Find one of my tapes, and see how I prayed for you."

At that moment, Eric tapped on the door. "You are tired," he said. "Let me take Rafe in and show him the books."

"Show him my press books, too, will you? So he can confound Emily. Goodbye, Mr. Pierce. I wish you well."

"And I you, Miss Watson." He looked even more awkward and uncertain than he had before, and she wondered if she had introduced any new ideas into his shuttered mind.

When they left, she leaned hard against the pillows. She was tired beyond belief—what had she done that her people should send her such stressful meetings? But she shook away the self-pitying thought.

She had, no doubt of it, faults and failings. She had been too busy to examine them, over the years, but now there was time. Perhaps she could mend her faults and become a better and a wiser person, before the end. She had been filled with unbelief and rebellion, when the first symptoms of her illness made themselves felt. Limbs schooled in the most precise obedience suddenly would not function as she wanted. Her breath, conditioned for years, became unreliable. Her heart, the steady engine propelling her body, had gone soggy and slow.

She'd bucked like an unbroken colt, thinking that more hours of schooling would reverse the thing happening to her body. She drove herself so hard that her fellow dancers had come to her at last, begging her to see the truth.

"You are kill yourself," Dmitri had told her. "And it is no good. We see how you push-push, and we see how you are pale and shaking at the end. The art, it is finish for you. Dance no more, Neelya, or you will dance with death."

His pale Russian eyes had been cool, but he had understood what he was asking. His hand on hers had shaken with emotion.

She had thought her efforts invisible to others, believing that she could drive by her will the flesh that had begun to fail her. But her dancers had been correct. She was fooling herself and cheating her public of the effortless ease that was her hallmark.

She talked with Boris the next day, putting into motion the transfer of direction for her troupe. She retired with much fanfare and no mention of her physical problem. She wanted no maudlin speeches at her last performance, and there had been none.

Since that night, she had learned to accept the unacceptable, though it had not been easy. She refused many aspects of her condition.

Hospitalization, artificial methods of prolonging her life were unacceptable. That much was hers to decide. But now she knew that she was completing the work begun when she was a child and began learning to control her strong young body. Now she must take over the conditioning of her mind and her spirit.

It was a matter of disciplining old habits out of existence, of making old ways of thinking turn new and fresh and constructive. She must go through to the end without bitterness and anger. She understood that with sudden clarity.

She rang the bell, and Amanda appeared. "Get you something, C'nelia?"

"Before Mr. Pierce goes, tell him"—her breath came short, and there was a great weight in her chest—"thank him for me. For coming. He made me realize some things that I needed to think about. Don't...let him think it has anything to do with the church. Say that he made me see my own faults. And I thank him for that."

Amanda nodded. With her quick perceptiveness, she seemed to grasp what Cornelia had felt. "I'll tell him. Now you rest, for Jonathan is coming tomorrow, and we want you to be able to visit with him."

Cornelia closed her eyes. Inside, she was busy thinking about her attitudes toward everything in her life, and before she knew it she was asleep.

CHAPTER FOURTEEN

ALLEYS CAN LEAD TO STRANGE THINGS

Cornelia lay against her pillows, watching as Amanda changed the painting on the wall facing her. The tall, narrow watercolor glowed with color as careful hands straightened it a last time and the older woman stepped back to study it.

"Brings back memories," she murmured, and Cornelia nodded. It did, indeed. She knew the artist well, for he had been a great admirer of her work.

His dark watercolor, splashed with light from the standard above the stage door, showed the alley just outside the theater where her troupe had rehearsed. The stage door was open, and through it could be seen a glimpse of scenery.

A dancer in black and white was caught in miniature through a gap in the curtains, her attitude, delicate as a poised butterfly, faithfully reproduced as the painter saw it from the rear and at an angle.

"Letitia," said Cornelia. "You can't see her face, but he got her body perfectly. See how she holds her hands? And that free ankle—just the perfect position. She was such a wonderful dancer...is such a wonderful dancer.

"I seem to feel that because my own life is about to stop, everyone else's has come to a halt, as well. Ego is a hard thing to defeat, Amanda."

"Be that as it may, you need a quick wash and brush up before the doctor gets here. It's almost time, and Jonathan likes to sit and talk."

"And enjoy Ella's cookies and pies," Cornelia said, smiling.

She was weary, even after sleeping with drugged intensity for eleven hours. But she struggled up to sit on the edge of her bed for a moment. Then she used her walker to make her way to the reclining chair by the window. As she sank into its depths, she could hear Amanda bustling about the bed.

Below her window was a young althea bush, whose pink blossoms were still coming and going regularly. Beyond was the big ash tree, surrounded by clipped grass.

She gazed out for a moment at a hummingbird drinking from a feeder. Then she took her notebook from the table beside her. As Lucius suggested, she was writing anecdotes from her career as she thought of them. The editor who had already accepted the book would put her material into order.

THE LIFE OF THE HEART she wrote in neat capitals at the top of the page. She tapped her chin with the ballpoint, thinking of the birth of that ballet.

The idea had come to her years before, after she worked (amid tempests and conflict) with Balanchine. She had put it aside, knowing that she was not yet mature enough to do it justice. And at last its time had come, after she organized her own troupe.

"In creating this group of dances, I was most fortunate in having a number of dancers of stellar quality," she began.

She listed their names, recalling as she did so each person's peculiar stamp on her memory. Letitia, never satisfied with her own performance. Daniel, whose movements could strike sparks in anyone watching. Fourteen people, all of whom had shared with her the birth of a tiny bit of the truth she had pursued all of her life.

She wrote busily, trying to get onto paper all the things that made each of those dancers important and unique. She was amazed when Amanda touched her shoulder.

"The doctor's here. Let's get you back into bed, so you can rest while you talk with him. You've got...my Lord, you've done a big chunk in that notebook! I'd better get out another, just in case."

Jonathan's brisk step tapped along the hallway. "And how is my patient?" he asked. "I'd have been here sooner, but we had a broken arm at the playground. Always something!"

He perched on the rocker and looked at her closely. He didn't make any motion toward examining her today...they both knew the futility of that.

She could tell by his expression that he was saddened by the change in her since he last came. At this point, she knew too well, a few days made terrible inroads into her strength.

"Medication still working well? No disorientation?"

"It's doing the job for me. I want to thank you for that. I was prepared to die the hard way, without any painkiller, but you saved me from it. It will probably mean my book will be finished, or almost, when I go."

He glanced at the stack of notebooks beside the bed and the smaller pile beside the recliner. "You have been busy!"

"I have, indeed. Even finding Mom's journals hasn't delayed me by much." She glanced up at the painting.

"Jonathan, look at that watercolor up there. What does it say to you?" She waited with interest as he turned to gaze at the picture.

When he looked back at her, his eyes were curiously alight. "The theater has always had a peculiar magic for me. My grandfather was a theater addict, and he took me backstage to meet several actresses for whom he had great admiration.

"I was a child, at the time. But that alley...and the stage door...and the glimpse of the stage beyond...they bring back the feelings I used to have, as if I were going behind the looking glass or into an enchanted door that came out into fairyland."

"Would you believe that I came the nearest I will ever come to finding God beyond that door?"

He nodded, a short jerk of the chin. "I did, myself, several times. And you, who created some of the magic we saw, probably met the Maker of Magics more often than anyone else."

Cornelia smiled warmly. "You are a comfort, Jonathan. I thought that Eric was the only person who could ever tune into my somewhat rarefied wavelength. But you do it so well

I almost suspect you of having an eccentric sister hidden away someplace."

He grinned. "Not hidden away. Big as life, and just about as bewildering. She's a professor of psychology at the University, married to a fellow who never knows what to make of her, and when she needs to talk she tracks me down. We've been known to talk all night, on the few occasions when I don't get called away to deliver babies or tend to broken arms."

He looked at her intently. "You have been remembering things that happened there?" He jerked his chin toward the picture. "Tell me!"

Cornelia closed her eyes. She could see the dimness backstage, smell the peculiar musty odor of sweat and flowers and dust that distinguishes old theaters. She could hear the record-player that replaced the piano as she worked out the individual segments of her *chef d'œuvre*.

"Each dancer followed a single melodic element, played by one instrument. I couldn't use the piano, because it made it too difficult for the dancers to distinguish their parts. We used taped recordings, made for us by friends of the composer, because I could not afford to hire union musicians for choreographic sessions."

She could hear the music. Around her, Daniel was leaping to match the soaring notes of the French horn; Letitia was doing a series of *fouettes*, keeping perfect time to the piping of a flute.

She was working with Elena, the youngest of the troupe, at the *enchainement* linked to the violins. When the child had grasped the feel of the steps, Cornelia stepped back to observe the effect of this part of *La Vie du Coeur*.

She moved across the barn-like rehearsal room and sat to watch. As the music wove its tapestry, the individual elements of the dances began to mesh.

She could see that the lips of the dancers were no longer moving, counting. They had worked their bodies into the fabric of the piece, the counts now a part of them.

The music wove them into tighter and tighter configurations, closely matched rhythmic patterns. The throbbing motif moved through all the parts of the orchestration, and the

102

group pulled into a pattern of linked bodies that seemed to throb, too, in an approximation of blood rhythms.

Sitting there, watching the thing that had been in her mind being born in living flesh, Cornelia felt something huge and almost frightening inside herself. Awe? Perhaps. Almost terror, though that was not an accurate term for it.

WHO AM I, TO MEDDLE WITH THE STUFF OF LIFE?

A silent voice spoke inside her, welling up from some unsuspected place within her spirit. She had thought that surgeons might feel so, but it had never occurred to her that what she did manipulated the spirit and the mind as drastically as the scalpel altered the tissues of the body.

She had sat, watching the final convulsive movements, each dancer responding to the dying notes of his or her instrument, the whole group folding upon itself into an amorphous shape that did, indeed, resemble a human heart. The grouping pulsed, slowing, slowing, slowing at last to a stop.

She found the time to think gratefully of Arthur Morton, her composer. He understood exactly what she wanted and needed. He had given her a brilliant piece of work.

Then she was on her feet, applauding. Letitia came to peer at her through her own sweat. "We weren't that good," she said, her voice disapproving.

"Far from perfect," Cornelia agreed. "But it has something...something that is going to move people, I think. Tomorrow we will really begin to work on it. When we add the Spirit of Life motif, it will truly be something. It will make our season, if I'm not mistaken."

The doctor touched her hand, and she opened her eyes to smile at him. Something of the magic of that moment was still with her, lingering through the intervening years.

"And did it ever!" he said. "My grandfather used to take the *Saturday Review of Literature*, and they had an entire Dance section devoted to that ballet. I suspect that ballet is still in production, somewhere."

"Everywhere," she agreed. "I hear regularly from companies that want advice as to the staging and the precise positions of even such tiny elements as fingers and chins. Labanotation—don't frown; that is a sort of musical notation for dance—is a wonderful thing, but it just gives the major movements of arms and legs and backs and heads. It cannot convey nuances.

"I have the film we made, you know. I make copies for anyone who asks. This may well be my immortality."

"Few have one with such impact. I saw that film. You remember Christmas—when?—four or five years ago, when PBS presented it?"

"And did it say anything special to you? I have wondered what a doctor might think of it," Cornelia said, raising her head.

She felt a surge of excitement. After all the years, talking about that work still moved her strongly.

"It said that here is a spirit that loves life and all who live it. It said that whatever we do, heal bodies, make dances, clean streets, cobble shoes, or grow food, we are all elements of the life of the heart. And we all come together at the end, spirit to spirit, body to soil. There is nothing to fear; that is what it said to me. Strongly."

Cornelia felt tears at the corners of her eyes. She sighed unconsciously. What she had felt was not her imagination. She had grasped, just for an instant, a truth, and she had been able to capture it and convey it to others. What a wonderful thing that was!

"I had to learn that the hard way," Jonathan said, still staring at the painting. "If I had seen your work before I interned, it would have helped me. As it was, I had to put fear behind me, refuse it house-room.

"Fear can warp your judgment, and for a doctor that can be deadly. But I often felt it knocking away at the door behind which I confined it."

"I did the same with pain," she said, nodding her understanding. "My right hip became infected, many years ago. It was treatable, but the surgery left some sort of scar tissue or bone spur or something of the sort.

"They told me that I could not dance. It would be too painful. But I told them that I would dance. It was worth the pain. So for the last eight years of my career, I was accompanied by discomfort that added, I think, something extra to my work. And it was, indeed, worth it."

He stared at her, his head cocked. "Why am I not surprised?" he asked her. "And of course that gave you the necessary conditioning for handling this illness as you have. You had a course of training for it." He rose and shook his head.

"Now you had better rest. Amanda told me that you've been writing steadily all morning. That's good. Keeps your mind off things. But you still have to rest and eat, or you won't get that other sort of truth onto paper in time." He looked sad.

"I think, even after so short an acquaintance, you will be sorry to see me go," she said. "But you shouldn't be. It will be such a relief to me."

"I know. I know. But this has brought back a lot of memories I had stored away in my mental attic. I hadn't thought of my grandfather in a long time. I hadn't recalled *Life of the Heart*, either. Why did you change it from the French?"

"Because we live in a nation of linguistic illiterates. They seem to be frightened of other tongues, and I wanted this to speak to everyone I could interest. I felt that it had a lot to say, not in words but in...what? Primitive eidola?"

"That will do until you find a better term." He looked back toward the picture. Then he glanced down at his wristwatch. "Got to go. Even on my day off, I have to check in with my patients at the hospital."

She took his offered hand and squeezed it. "Why in the world do you waste your precious time off on a swollen old hulk like me?"

"Because, Cornelia Watson, you wake up my mind. You bring back to me many things that I should never forget. And you make my heart come to life with a new perceptiveness. I am a better doctor for knowing you. I would come more often, if it were not so far and I were not so busy. I treasure our talks, believe me."

She lay back. Warmth filled her, and comfort. As he walked away, talking quietly with Amanda, she marveled that it was possible to help others, even at the edge of her own death.

Life was, indeed, a marvelous mystery.

CHAPTER FIFTEEN

THE TANGLED TRAIL OF DREAM

She drifted into a light sleep. Through its tenuous web, she could hear the mockingbird in the ash tree, the vibrant hum of the hummingbirds' wings, and the creaking of locusts in the edge of the wood.

All those elements spun themselves together and blurred. She shrank away from the world she knew into another, no less real and far more intriguing.

She hung in blackness. Velvety, impalpable, depthless. *Am I a planet?* she asked herself. *A dark star, moving through space?*

There was no answer, but she hadn't expected any. Instead, she felt motion. There was no air, so that did not betray movement. No wind touched her body or her face. There was no background rushing past, yet she knew she was moving swiftly. Through space or through time? There was no way to know.

Trusting herself to that dark immensity, she let herself flow with the current that was bearing her away from the swollen body she had grown to hate, the room that was a pleasant prison, the house she still loved, and the forest that wrapped it round.

She went into a timeless, breathless place, where she had no body but was able to move as freely as only the bodiless can manage to do.

Then she saw the stars. Not as distant specks, occluded by haze or cloud or pollution, but as great burning chunks of elemental matter, caught in the webs of gravity, moving in ever-expanding patterns.

They swarmed about her as if she were surrounded by a flight of fireflies, though the motions were orderly and precise. She caught her nonexistent breath in wonder and delight.

She worried, as she moved into the patterns, about disrupting orbits, tearing the intricate web apart. But she seemed to have no body, no gravity of her own.

She could dance among the stars as one of themselves, yet without upsetting any element of their choreography. She had dreamed, from time to time for all of her life, of being freed so, without the limitations of gravity or musculature or flesh to drag her down.

She spun in space, feeling with some esoteric sense the suns striking through whatever served as her physical self. Swirls of cosmic dust looped about her shoulders, like some immense shawl, sequined with motes of light. She moved faster, thrusting tenuous arms through galaxies, bending to feel systems touch her lips like mist.

She was happy. Happier than she could recall being in her entire life. She was dancing the Great Choreography that formed the universe, knowing within herself all the multitudes of truths required for that formation.

She had no limitations. She could drift with the freedom of an atom, spin with the swiftness of a star, leap from nothingness to nothingness without fear of failure or falling. Such mastery was a thing that had touched her only in her dreams.

Still she moved, through looping galaxies, bright trails of comets, whirlpooled nebulae...toward the fringes of the thronged universe, toward a small yellow sun on the edge of a sparse galaxy. Toward home.

Huge as she was, she greeted that far-farer as an equal. The orbits of its attendant worlds were about her, as she shrank, dropping into their pattern. Mercury warmed his winged heels in the embrace of the star. Venus rose from a sea of space. Terra...she dropped quickly, now, shrinking still more.

She was smaller than the planet, than the moon, becoming a hurtling fragment, a meteor that tracked through the sky toward the dark half of the sphere below her. She felt no heat, no sensation of friction, though she knew she would have, if she had possessed mass. A sadness filled her, as she neared the gravity-ridden surface of her home.

There would be no more spinning freely through the clouds of stars. No leaping across galaxies. Only that grossly swollen body awaited her, dying. What a fearful thing it was to return to it!

She opened her eyes. It was dark outside the window. The ash tree was black against the spangled sky. She greeted those points of light with regret.

"I'll dance with you again," she murmured. Then she woke fully and found her brother beside the bed, rocking gently in the small rocking chair. The lamp was not burning. The only light came from the hallway, and in its dim glow she could see that he was worried, even as he slept. When she sighed and reached to touch his hand, he started.

"Neely? You awake now?" His voice was soft, almost fearful.

"I went so far," she breathed. "And it was so hard to come back. So hard. I'd like to have stayed where I was."

Eric swallowed hard. She could hear the gulping sound. "We thought, for a while, that you weren't going to. Come back, I mean. I didn't want you to go without someone here, and neither did Amanda. She's over there in the recliner."

Cornelia hardly heard his words. She was trying to paint for them a picture of her own, with words. "I was out there." She waved toward the ash tree and the stars beyond it. "I was one of them. Not small. Huge! Weightless, not physical at all.

"But I could dance. I could dance, with all the gold and green and lavender and pink fires burning around me, spinning through space, making wheels within wheels, all across the cosmos. And the darkness was as beautiful as the light, deep and velvety and awesome.

"I swam in it like a fish in the sea. I danced in it like a butterfly in the wind. I was free. Altogether free. No weight. No up or down. No limitations at all."

Amanda held a glass to her lips, and she sipped cool water. When it was gone, she said, "I never was afraid of dying.

108

Curious, not afraid. Now I look forward to it so much...so much! And not just to get away from this...thing. To go back. Back there...."

Amanda came again, this time with medicine. She swallowed it obediently, but her mind was still out there, where she had found freedom. She slipped again into sleep, still longing to dance among the stars.

But this time her dream was different. She walked down the street in the painting that had already been removed, along the peaceful street in the morning mist, beneath that silver-apple sun.

She knew who lived in each house. She was old, not middle-aged and sick but elderly and in fair health. She could feel her bones creak as she moved, her muscles protesting painfully. She didn't find it unpleasant. Merely familiar, like the sounds an old house makes in a windstorm.

There the Mosbeys lived. Paul and Deborah and Sallie Vee and John. They were young and busy. The children were noisy but usually well behaved, and they were not afraid of old people, as some tended to be. She gave them dancing lessons, sometimes, on her own front porch.

Early as it was, small John was on the Victorian veranda, waiting for her. Every morning she walked around the four-block square. To stop walking would be to let her body freeze up like an old car left sitting for too long. Often the child went with her on her round.

She waved, and he rose from the swing and came bouncing across the dew-webbed lawn to her side. In the summer, he managed to walk most of the way with her, being the only one of the children who still woke with the dawn. "Miss Watson! Miss Watson! There's the biggest old cotton spider in the four-o-clock bushes!"

She smiled down. "I have one, too. They like those best, I think. I suspect they take naps in the flowers, along with the elves."

He never took her hand, being too independent for such things. But he was very good about staying beside her and never dashing out into the streets ahead of her.

His literal mind was struggling with her words. "Maybe the spider does, but there's not really elves. Not truly. Are there?" He stared up with round black eyes. She thought he might become a lawyer or an engineer, so material was his way of thinking. "I used to think that. But now that I'm very old and have better vision, I think there must be. It would make me sad to think there were not."

He knitted fine dark brows. "Daddy says elves and fairies and ghosts are stitious lusions. He won't let me look at books that have stories about them. So I'd better not."

"Not do what?" She looked down curiously.

"Not look in the flowers to see."

"I suspect that would be best. We wouldn't want to wake up a stitious lusion from his nap, would we?" She chuckled.

But he was stooping, his dark mop of hair almost touching the grass beside the walk. A line of ants had organized an expedition to a crumb of dropped cookie on the next lawn.

With great care, he was diverting the latter half of the column, sweeping the insects aside with a twig. The ants there were milling in confusion, though the front of the train still marched toward its goal.

Cornelia felt with sudden clarity just how the diverted ants must feel. Lost from their secure rank, the order of their universe destroyed, they were searching frantically for some order to bring them out of the chaos. She had once known such chaos, herself....

When? She could not recall it clearly, but she was quite certain of it.

"Let them be, John. How would you like for someone to push us aside off the walk and make us have to search and search to find our way home?"

He squatted beside the ants, looking up at her. His dark head was cocked on one side, as he considered her question. Then he rose to brush off the seat of his pants. "Wouldn't like it," he said. "You think they mind?"

"Not if you let them find their way again and go about their business. They'll take bits of that cookie back into the anthill and feed it to the queen, did you know that?" They walked slowly onward, as she racked her brain for everything she had ever read about ants and the life of the hill. He was such a reasonable little fellow—she was sorry his father

110

had superstitious delusions of his own. Imagination was the balm that made living in the real world bearable, she had often thought.

Now they were coming back along the other side of the block where she took her morning walk. Her bones protested, as they usually did, at her inhumane treatment of an eighty-year-old body.

They came to the circular bench around the Clarks' white oak, and she sat, as usual, to rest for a bit. The paper boy had already passed on his round, and the going-to-work traffic had not yet begun.

John's quiet babble harmonized with the chirping of a mockingbird in the oak. It was always nice, here. Her old life of dancing and teaching was now so distant it seemed like a dream.

She could see her house in the distance, and she blessed the young couple who rented the upstairs and looked after her as part of their payment. She was respected by her neighbors, who didn't dream that Miss Watson, who willingly sat with sick children or made herb teas for sniffly adults, had been the great Cornelia Watson. That was just as she liked it.

Her family was gone, even her much younger sister. She might be alone in the world in that sense, but she never felt it. Keeping busy kept her healthy, and she was content with her life.

John said, "It's almost time for brekfuss. Better go."

She smiled and creaked to her feet, as he ambled ahead of her. The mist had burned almost away. The sun had turned from silver to red-gold as it climbed through the branches of the trees. The street's cool blue-gray had warmed with sunlight, as had the roofs of the houses, rose and blue and bottle-green.

"It's a lovely world," she murmured.

But John was forging ahead, his stomach ready for food. His mind had discarded ants and ancient dancers alike, as he headed for his breakfast. He peeled up his own walk with a flip of his hand for farewell.

She turned toward her house. Trudging up the wide steps, she felt her knees pop. Oh, for the time when she could go up into a *tour jeté* with ease and grace!

She laughed—and woke. It was morning; rain was tickling the leaves outside her window. The ash tree was a gray ghost, and the wood beyond the fence was lost in a silver curtain of raindrops.

Eric was asleep beside the bed, his head bent uncomfortably against the back of the rocker.

"Wake up, sleepyhead," she said. "You're going to have a terrible crick in your neck!"

He opened his eyes and yawned. Then he grinned. "Good morning. You slept!"

"And dreamed," she said, remembering the peace of her vision. "And dreamed!"

Chapter Sixteen

Unexpected Journey

The rain stopped during the night, and Cornelia woke the next morning feeling better than she had in weeks. Eric and Amanda were astonished at her vigor, as she ate a fair breakfast, finished a stint of writing, sent the pages off with Amos to be photocopied, and wheeled her chair through the house to the porch.

"I want to go to the woods," she said, after lunch. "I may never feel well enough again. I want you to take me up the lane and go away and leave me for an hour or two. "I never had the time, when I was home for a visit or at Dad's funeral. That is the thing I missed most, while I was away. Now there is one thing I badly need to do, though I didn't think I was going to make it. But today I can, and I'm going to."

She piled argument on argument, as she saw refusal take shape on their faces. But by the time she was done with her plea, she could see that Eric understood what it was she wanted. He, too, was a woods wanderer. He, too, liked to commune with the forest alone.

His eyes met hers and he nodded. "I know. We'll take you, won't we Amanda?"

"Take her out into the woods with all the wild beasts I hear screaming in the night? Leave her there to be eaten by bobcats and mosquitoes?" Amanda sounded shocked. Cornelia laughed until she hurt. "Mosquitoes, dear. Not bobcats. They have better manners, not to mention taste."

Eric patted Amanda's shoulder. "We'll be close by. If she meets a bear, she can yell, and we'll come running."

113

"In which direction?" Amanda's tone was dry. "I don't want to meet any bears, or bobcats either. But I guess if you two are set on it, I'll have to go along. I think I'll take my knitting. Those needles are good weapons, if I should need something."

It was hot, but not muggy and humid, as East Texas Julys sometimes become. Warmth struck through Cornelia's bones, as Eric pushed her chair down the lane leading from the back yard into the forest. The uneven ground vibrated her chair, but it was not as painful as it might have been.

Once beneath the oaks and pines and hickories, it was cooler. The light was greenish, slashed with shafts of harsh gold where the sun struck through the canopy of leaves. A clump of ironwort mirrored her earlier dream, and goldenrod rose, a bright column, above it.

The pines here stood far apart, dark-needled amid the lighter greens. A woodpecker was at work, his tok-toking providing counterpoint to the songs of birds. "Pretty-girl, pretty-girl," sang a cardinal, beneath the cadenza of an orchard oriole.

Even Amanda was wide-eyed, as they trundled along the path to the clearing Cornelia remembered, in the heart of the wood. One side was bounded by hawthorns, the other three by sweet gum saplings and hickories. In the middle was a huge chunk of rock, which she now knew must have been a meteorite, by its shape and color.

The clearing was shady, and she halted her procession there. "You and Amanda go and see about the hickory nut crop, or pick flowers, or play word games. I want to stay here for a while. Give me plenty of time, if you can."

They looked at each other, then at her. "We'll go back to the house and watch the clock," Eric said.

She smiled with relief. "If that's what you want. And don't worry. Nothing here can hurt me, except my own body. And if that should happen, and I die here in the middle of the wood, it would be the most wonderful way to go that I can imagine. Thank you."

"You should have been one of the Babes in the Wood," he said. "Come on, Amanda. We're not wanted. I'll play you a game of Scrabble, how about that?"

The old woman grunted irritably, but she put a hand on Cornelia's shoulder for a moment before following him up the path.

When the last sound of quiet steps crackled into silence, Cornelia closed her eyes. She listened with all her might, as she had done in the forest since she was a child. She had learned at an early age all the voices of the wood, and now recognition came back to her easily. Breeze flipped a leaf someplace high overhead. A nearby pine sighed in breathy rasps. Birds of a dozen kinds twittered or sang or chattered, resting through the hot afternoon.

A squirrel scolded in the distance, and she heard something fall from above. An acorn or a pine cone, perhaps, hit branch after branch as it clattered toward the ground.

So many sounds, so many voices, all rooted in her childhood. She heard a sigh, a scuffling of leaves, and she turned her head cautiously.

A pointed face looked at her from a screen of hawthorns. If she had not known what to look for—and how to look!—she would never have detected the doe, gazing out at her.

She sat watching, being watched. Then the deer was gone, as silently as if she had dissolved. Cornelia sighed, turning the chair to survey the small glade. The track at the farther edge seemed fairly smooth, and she pushed herself toward it. She conserved her strength as well as she could, but the morning's energy seemed to be holding.

In that narrow way, her elbows brushed leafy growth on either side. She managed to make her way until she reached another spot she remembered. There the path forked, and in that angle was a low spot, in which jacks-in-the-pulpit bloomed in the spring. Only traces of leaves and stalks showed they still kept their yearly vigil.

"There are some things that never change," she said. A jaybird shot off a branch above her with an indignant squawk. "Even jaybirds!" she called after him.

For whatever reason, she felt young today. Strong. Happy. She turned so she could look down both angles of the path. Sitting quietly, breathing as silently as she could, she waited until the living creatures about her forgot she was there. Motion rippled in dead leaves beyond the path. A

115

coachwhip glided onto the dust, across, flicking its dark length quickly out of sight in the mulch of the wood. Something moved toward her from deeper in the trees, and the scufflings hinted at something large.

She waited, bent forward with anticipation. Would she see another deer? The sound came nearer, but she could see nothing. Then she understood the movement was at ground level.

Bobbing heads, each with a neat white stripe along their sides, betrayed a covey of quail, scratching along as leisurely as a flock of hens. They talked quietly in murmurs and chirps as they passed, without seeing her motionless form at all.

Hardly had she recovered from that when a squirrel flirted down the bole of the hickory beside her. She didn't move. He leaped the last ten feet to the ground to scrabble among the leaves and come up with an ancient nut. His tiny hands turned it over. Then he dropped it in disgust and turned to look directly into her eyes.

The creature froze in its tracks, but she made no motion, almost stopped breathing. It cocked its head, flirted its tail again, and was gone up the tree almost too quickly to see.

A gusty sigh, just behind her, almost made her jump out of the chair. She wheeled to see an ancient mule standing in the path, regarding her with eyes in which shone the wisdom of the ages. Black from nose to tail, he was sprinkled with the silver hairs of age.

"Coaly?" she asked, hardly daring to hope. The Coaly she had known as a feisty four-year-old could hardly be alive. Or could he? Mules sometimes lived to be over thirty years old.

"Coaly?" She held out a hand, and he dropped his head to stare at it.

He lifted a heavy hoof to come nearer, snorting softly. The wrinkled velvet of his nose touched her fingers. He sighed again, his warm breath tickling her fingers.

"You old devil! You'll outlast us all. You're too wise to die." She laughed softly, and he rolled one dark eye to examine her.

116

She had shelled corn for him, after his long days working in the field. The iron sheller, the rattle of corn raining into the bucket came back to her sharply.

He raised his head and looked down the path, as if something had called him. Without another glance, he went away, stamping out the print of the snake's passing. As a parting gift, he dropped a string of dung-balls in the track.

"Just like a mule," Cornelia said aloud. She looked up through the hickory leaves into the dust-blue sky. The sun was slanting, now. She pushed, sending the chair back toward the other clearing.

Partway along, she stopped as a terrapin trundled across the trail, pushing a bow-wave of leaves ahead of him. His wrinkled face, held arrogantly high, withdrew into the shell at once when he saw her.

She moved closer and lifted him, looking into the slit at the front of his shell. He glared back at her, indignant at being manhandled by a giant. She set him carefully in the dead leaves. She hadn't looked a terrapin in the face in forty years, and she was glad to have had one last chance.

The wood was dimming as the sun moved westward. The treetops were brilliant with light, but the shadows were already foreshadowing twilight among the thick foliage. Tree frogs were already beginning their shrill chirring, and a whip-poor-will was tuning up in the wood.

A drift of cooler air moved the bushes, and the pines sighed more deeply. With amazing suddenness, the katydids began their raucous kazooing, seeming to fill the trees. The sound brought back memories of summer evenings, sitting in the yard with her mother, shelling peas or snapping beans...

"Cornelia!"

She sprang back into the present as Eric and Amanda came into sight around a bend in the path. They looked anxious; she had known they would. But dying alone was not as terrible as people seemed to think, she was almost certain.

For an instant, the relief on their faces made them look exactly alike.

"Ridiculous to worry about me," she said. "But I am tired."

As they wheeled her away, she didn't look back. She had no need to, for she carried with her the forest's infinite detail, safely stored away in the part of her that she knew to be immortal.

Chapter Seventeen

Traces in the Dust

She paid, of course, for her day of freedom. Cornelia had known she would, but it was worth it, and she never complained of the pain that wracked her, the next morning. Each joint seemed to possess its own tone and pitch, while her heart slogged along, feeling as if it might give up its efforts at any moment. The medication dulled the symphony of pain to a bearable point no more. The energy that gave her the time in the woods was gone as if it had never existed.

Eric sat beside her bed until she shooed him away. "There's no use in having both of us miserable," she told him. "Go and do something interesting. All our Puritan ancestors would zap you if you did something that was fun while your sister is dying, but do find something useful, like locating more of Mom's stories. I am going to ignore the way I feel and work on the book."

"You can't sit up to write!" he protested.

"No, but I can lie here and talk into the tape recorder Lucius brought me, for the time when I couldn't write. Now scoot—I'm going to work."

When he left, she lay back against the pillows and set the tiny machine beside her on the table. Before snapping it on, she gazed out past the ash tree, into the forest that was now too distant for her to reach, ever again. There and in the acres beyond it, she had begun to search for her place in the universe. A small figure in faded jeans, she had trudged along that track, carrying a book and a sandwich in her knapsack, heading for the trees. Beyond the wood there was a tract of young pines, back then, in a field eroded so badly that it was put into trees to stabilize it. The branches swept almost to the ground, and beneath them was a smooth carpet of dry needles.

She'd loved to crawl beneath a special pine that grew on the edge of a small creek. She would lie in the cool shade, listening to the trickle of water and watching the sun make patterns of shadow about her; when she grew tired of watching and listening, she'd read.

She had been perhaps ten years old when the cardinal talked to her. She might have been dozing, perhaps, when the bird perched on the dead branch above her. Cocking its head, it focused its black eyes on her with such a knowledgeable expression that she was certain it meant to tell her something.

"Hello, redbird," she said softly.

Its round eye blinked once, and the head turned to cock in the other direction. Having examined her with its right eye, it brought the left to bear.

She whistled a quiet trill, and the bird replied with a complicated series of notes. She tried to imitate that, but she lost track after a few measures.

That didn't bother the cardinal, who proceeded to talk with her, very politely, for what seemed a long time. When he tired of it, the bird hopped to a higher branch, preened for a moment, and flew. She lay back, letting her gaze move up through the needled limbs to the sky above the treetop.

She'd learned something, though she had no way of knowing what it might be. She just knew that a complete world required Cornelia, this pine tree, and a bird like that cardinal.

Now, lying in her bed at the end of her life, she thought about that and could find no disagreement in her. Man might think himself master of the world, but other elements were even more necessary than he. Even the snakes were a vital part of this natural world, though she couldn't feel she'd ever grow friendly with them.

The cows on the farm? They weren't wild and natural, of course. They had traded their freedom for food and protection from wolves and weather. She felt a bit of distaste, thinking of that. But they were too placid and unthinking to mind it.

There were things her kind did that she knew were useful and also ugly. Man thought he was the master of the universe, but nobody she knew could halt a tornado. Nobody could make it rain when the weather turned dry. Earthquakes and landslides were outside the control of anybody.

She had heard many of her neighbors talk of owning their land, but she thought her father had the better notion. He said that he held it in trust for the future. Anyone cutting all the trees or ruining the land was cheating nature, he had told her. That was one of the ugly things.

But then there were music and painting and dance, and those were the things that, like the cardinal, her species did for the glory of it all. Why did people like her aunt feel so threatened by things that spoke to the spirit, without regard for the church or the pocketbook? She had never resolved that question.

She realized that she had turned on the tape, and her musings had been recorded. Good. Her editor could take out what he felt was unnecessary, but some of it probably explained why she had become the person she was. And if nothing else, it had brought back one of her most pleasant memories from her childhood.

Perhaps that was her secret base, from which she had thrust up her unique set of talents. All the artists she had known, whatever the field in which they worked, seemed to share a secret they could not put into words. Only through exercising their arts could they convey it to others.

She knew the feeling well, for it was her own compulsion. And even now, on the edge of death, she found no words with which to make it clear.

From time to time, when she and Eric were closest, she felt he must know such a vital thing, but she understood that, if asked, he would have no better answer than she did. Perhaps the answer did not fit into words at all. "It well may be," she said into the machine, "that for each individual there is a different secret, together with a different compulsion toward sharing. This might explain the variety of arts and of artists.

"We all have a wonderful thing, unique to us. Some of us realize it and try bringing it out through nonverbal means. At this point, after years and experience have taught me, I wonder if that is not one of the subliminal statements given through The Life of the Heart: All hearts, each different in chemistry and emotion, beat to a common rhythm and aspire to a common goal."

Cornelia paused and turned off the recorder. She must think clearly, now. She wanted to say something with great effectiveness.

Her electric fan whirred softly, and she blessed this mild summer that had not demanded air conditioning. In the distance she heard Ella's glass wind chimes, tinkling in the light breeze on the porch. Words came into her mind, and she spoke again into the machine.

"I understand, now, that I have been learning, all along the way. I shudder to think of those who must learn those hard-won truths through trial and error, when I might give them the answer, if only there were words for it. It is a terrific secret, so simple nobody would believe it.

"For it merely gives you a way to live without hurting others. For enjoying what you have without yearning vainly for what you cannot possess. For finding joy in the smallest and least dramatic of things.

"If my kind could learn these things, we might begin moving toward maturity. And yet....

"It might be that only in the learning can the virtue be found. Knowledge may only be usable for those who have expended their own sweat and blood in gaining it. Perhaps knowledge attained effortlessly is worthless, for to know something with all your being, you must have experienced it.

"I cannot grieve that my work, dedicated to conveying the indescribable, has succeeded only minimally, if at all. I had, if nothing else, the joy of creating it. Those with whom I worked have had the pleasure of bringing it into being from that hidden world inside my mind. Those who have enjoyed the motion and the music, without exploring more deeply, seem to have been satisfied with the experience, and those who caught a glimpse of the thing I was trying to convey are welcome to use it as they will.

"I have worked very hard and found much pleasure in my labors. Perhaps that is the most vital thing there is, and it is never easy if you give all you are to your efforts. If it were easy, it would be worthless.

"Only in challenging the impossible can we be fully alive, fully human, possessed of the wonder of creation."

She rewound the tape and listened. It seemed to her she had made a certain amount of sense, and she wrote the label out and matched the number with that of a page in her notebook. "For Lucius," she wrote. "You might suggest that this contains a statement most suitable for ending the book. Even if I don't make it through the entire manuscript, this would be an appropriate ending."

She set aside the recorder and the notebook and leaned her head back on the pillows. She was tired, but the terrible, weighted weariness had withdrawn, for the time being.

She sighed and stretched. Her limbs moved sluggishly but without terrible discomfort. Amanda must have been listening for the rustle of the sheets, for she popped into the room.

"Need anything, C'nelia?"

Cornelia reached for the thin hand and squeezed it. "Do you feel you have learned, in the course of your life, something really vital and important, but you can't find words to make it clear to others?" she asked.

Amanda's fingers tightened about hers. "Yes, but it can't be done. More's the pity. As long as you don't know it can't, you keep trying. I've watched you, over the years, bursting with the effort to say the unsayable, and I've felt sorry for you. But now I know better, and I'm glad you didn't understand.

"What you did was worth all the effort and all the struggle. It's a pity...."

"What is?"

"That all too many people don't try, any more. I see youngsters, particularly, making it clear that anything they can't get without trying they'll never attempt. What a shame! They'll never amount to a pot of pitch, and they won't even know what they could have become, if only they'd tried."

She snorted. "Now I'll get down off my soapbox. But remember, you asked me!"

"I always get an honest answer. It's worth a mint. How long have you been taking care of me, Amanda?"

She frowned. "A long time. Let's not go counting years. Ever since the arthritis got too bad in my hands to let me sew for the troupe, that's how long."

"Thank heaven you took me on. What would I have done without you?"

Eric peered around the door. "You finished? How about lunch, and then a game of Scrabble?"

She smiled. He looked so young, even with gray hair and lined face. He was the one who had shared her childhood, and they had very little time left.

"I'd love to," she said.

Chapter Eighteen

The Way of the Old Ones

Cornelia's favorite painting had just been hung on the wall at the foot of her bed and straightened by Amanda's careful hands. The clear morning light struck through into the scene, freeing her, temporarily, from the burden of her illness.

A narrow track wound between cliffs that were marvels of rose and umber, with streaks of purest white where primordial beaches had left their sands. In the distance, through a notch between heights, there was a glimpse of sky, puffed with summer cloud, and a fragment of a valley. She knew that country. She had danced in Santa Fe and Taos many times, with her troupe. Once one of her hosts had driven her into those northern reaches, between cliffs striped like Christmas candy, over ridges that revealed beyond their backs long stretches of rolling countryside, stippled with vegetation and lined with canyons.

She had always wanted to follow one of those tracks that branched off the way, to go to the end, whatever that might be. But, as with all the other bypaths of her life, it had been left unexplored as she conquered the world of dance.

Now there was no more rigorous schedule demanding her time. Death, she found, was an unmapped road, leaving her the opportunity, if she had been able, to follow that rough track, to explore the canyons beyond the cliffs.

The illness had removed her doubts and inhibitions. "Why not?" she asked aloud. She had at least an hour before anyone would check on her again.

She wanted desperately to be out in the summer morning, smelling the air, hearing the birds. If she could not go in person, why not in imagination? She stared at the painting. The brushwork had formed those rocky declivities with exquisite accuracy. She could see the tough desert plants that had taken root along their bases and in crevices higher up. The track....

...was stony, beneath her boots. She could hear the crunch of her steps echoing away among the steep cliffs around her. The dry, sweet air invigorated her, filling her lungs, for the first time in months, with freely drawn breaths. She no longer felt waterlogged. She was in her dancer's body, not her dying flesh.

Swinging her arms, feeling the light knapsack on her back, she made her way along the base of the nearest cliff, rounding it as the trail turned. Beyond was a vista of more cliffs, bright with morning sun. Ahead, the track she followed forked, one very faint branch moving up the narrow canyon on her right.

The slot she traversed was still in shadow, but the sun was lighting the western heights to glory. The narrow way beside her was almost twilight-dark, for overhanging outcrops of stone shadowed it deeply.

A cottonwood guarded the entrance, and a thin trickle of water ran down a stony watercourse to lose itself in the larger channel that snaked down the big canyon. She could smell the sharp scent of wet stone and the indefinable odor of water that strikes through dry desert air. The coolness in the passage was pleasant, and she thought she smelled greenery ahead, as well.

She had read that such small canyons often held tiny valleys cut from the rock, watered by streams and filled with growing things. She knew that finding such a spot would set the seal of success on her expedition. A magpie came fluttering down the cleft toward her. As she came out from beneath the overhang, it saw her and banked sharply, darting upward with a shrill cry. Another, just behind it, followed it to a safe elevation, where they perched on a snag extending from the cliff and scolded her roundly.

She chuckled. The crisp black and white, the cheeky self-assurance of the birds amused her.

A narrow but adequate path edged the little stream. It was ochre-stained with runoff water, slick in spots, but quite passable. She walked along it, listening to the murmur of a breeze between the stony walls and the distant shriek of a hawk—or was that an eagle?—and the receding comments of the magpies. Beneath it all ran the voice of the water, tying everything together into a peaceful hum.

It was relatively cool in the shaded recesses where she moved. The sky above the narrow cleft was a blue so intense it seemed unreal.

She paused and picked up a handful of pebbles from the stream bed. Smoothed with the action of the water, they were deep rose and onyx and greenish-white, lovely as jewels. She put them into a pocket of her jacket and went on.

In the distance, she heard another note. Familiar. A dog barking? Did someone live in this enchanted place? She hurried forward, the stones clicking merrily in her pocket as she went. She found to her surprise that she had a staff in her hand—a good stout alpenstock, like those she had admired in Europe.

She used it to brace herself, as the path narrowed to a thin edge, just wide enough to hold a foot. Water, running down the face of the cliff beside her, made the stone slick.

She rounded the buttress that had forced the narrowing of the path and found herself on a much wider and better track. Just ahead, there was a deep pool, catching the little stream as it fell from some eight feet up over a lip of harder stuff.

A bucket sat beside the cup of rock. Another cottonwood leaned over it protectively, and a clump of pale blue blossoms was huddled very close to the verge.

Now the dog was very near. The barking roused terrific echoes, in fact, bouncing back and forth between the cliffs.

Cornelia went faster still, feeling something wonderful must lie around the twists and bends of the way. Somewhere in this canyon was something important to her that she needed to learn.

Now she could see the way had been smoothed. Larger stones had been removed and small ones had been used to fill in holes and runnels. In several places, a mallet had smashed off protruding bits of rock that could not be removed in any other way.

As she rounded a last protrusion, she found herself at the lower end of a lozenge-shaped valley. The walls receded to a distance of a quarter-mile apart, and the stream, shallow and shining in the light from above, glinted in the sunlight.

Cottonwoods grew thickly along the farther side of the stream, filling the cup to her left to the foot of the cliff. A thin fringe lined the nearer side, and a sort of jetty of rock thrust out into the water.

A woman knelt there, scrubbing vigorously at a garment, which she alternately rubbed with soap and pummeled against the rock in front of her. The dog, now quieter, ran to the woman, back toward Cornelia, then back to his mistress again, whining.

The woman wiped a wet arm across her forehead and looked up. Then she dropped the wet shirt and rose, with easy grace, to her moccasined feet.

Cornelia called across the distance between them, "Hello! I hope you don't mind my coming, but I was following this path, and it brought me here."

That didn't sound too intelligent, she thought, but the woman didn't seem to mind. She smiled, coming back along the line of stones to meet her unexpected guest. "You walk?" she asked. "Not many white people do. I expect you are thirsty?"

Cornelia nodded. "I have some water in my canteen, but it tastes nasty. I was afraid to try the water in the stream... you never know if it might be contaminated."

The woman smiled suddenly, her almond eyes unexpectedly merry. "Yes. There are cattle upstream. I would not wash clothes in the pool, if this were clean.

"I am Marita. Welcome to our home. We have little company, since my sons have grown and gone away. My father will be happy to see you...he gets lonely. Come to the house."

Cornelia looked around. She had not seen the house until that moment, for it was tucked into a nook of rock against the right-hand wall of the canyon.

It stood on a sort of shelf, some yards above the level of the valley, which she could tell from watermarks was above the water level when the snowmelt ran away downstream from the mountains beyond. Soil had been carried up, and pots and slop-jars and buckets held riots of moss rose and petunias and geraniums, springing in brilliant colors.

Before the stone and adobe-mud house was a long bench with a split log for a back. On it sat a man so old that ancient seemed too mild a term for him. He was watching her with eyes so bright and beady that she could see them spark, even before she and the woman reached the stone porch on which he waited.

Marita said something to her father in their own tongue. He looked toward her, then at Cornelia. "Welcome," he said, his old voice thin and reedy. "We do not see people often, since my grandsons went to school. What is it that a white woman seeks among these ancient stones?"

Cornelia didn't feel uncomfortable with the question. She wondered that, herself. While she considered her reply, she offered her hand. "I am Cornelia Watson. I am happy to meet you."

He smiled, revealing his lack of teeth, and shook her hand. His fingers were dry and wrinkled as withered twigs. "I am called Snow Mountain Man. I have seen many winters." She sat beside him as he indicated a spot. Marita went into the house, leaving the two to talk.

"You asked what I am seeking here," she began. "I hardly know. I have worked very hard, all of my life, looking for the truth at the heart of things. Now I am resting.

"I suspect I am looking for the truth at my own heart, and that is not easy to find. You must look in strange places, I am discovering."

"What is it that you work so hard to do?" he asked, with real interest in his seamed and weathered face.

"I dance."

He looked scornful, and she hastened to add, "Not in the way our young people dance, for pleasure. I dance the truths

I find, on the stage, and people pay me to do it, though I would dance whether I made money or not."

"In the white man's world, money is necessary," he admitted. "Show me."

Cornelia was startled. Dance? Here on this rough stone stage, beneath the crowning heights about them? Spotlighted by sun and the reflections off the water?

Why not?

"I must remove my boots," she said. "They are too stiff, and the soles are too rough."

She unstrapped them, loosed the laces, slid her feet free. The heavy socks would slip, she decided, and removed them, too, revealing her dancer's battered feet. Then she slipped off her bush jacket and tied the tails of her cotton shirt about her waist.

Marita, coming from the house with a pitcher and glasses, paused to watch as she did a brief warm-up exercise.

"This is not dance," Cornelia explained. "It makes my muscles flexible for dancing."

Snow Mountain Man nodded, his expression reserved. She sank onto the rock, full-length. Inside her, the initial theme from *Also Sprach Zarathustra* began to swell, and she grew upward from the stone like a flower seeking the light. Hands became leaves, finding freedom from the soil. They grew on stems that were her arms to cup the light and the water of the free air.

When she flowed upright, she found that freedom containing winds and winters. Those moved her body to their natural rhythms, twisting her, spinning her, blowing her, at last, in a *grand jeté*, away from the stone altogether.

"It is good," said Snow Mountain Man, when she sank onto the bench beside him. "It is real. You have found a truth, there, and I can see it. That is not easy to do, even with words. You have, I think, talked with the Old Ones."

"What Old Ones? I don't know what you mean."

"The Old Ones talk, and we do not always know. I think you have met them, though you did not understand that. I think they have told you some of their small secrets, and you made them into dance. It can be a good thing...sometimes." His tone was still a bit doubtful.

130

Marita interrupted them. "And now I know that you are thirsty. Probably hungry, too. I have made food ready. You like tortillas and beans? Come. It is not good to speak too freely of the Old Ones."

As she sipped from the glass, receiving one taste of the clear, pure water Marita offered her, Cornelia returned to her own place, there in the Monster Bed.

The taste of the spring water was still on her tongue. The scent of the canyon valley was in her nostrils. The feel of dancing was in her muscles.

But she was once again in her dying body. Not trapped...no, never trapped again. She had learned that, if nothing else, from the Old One whom she had met within her mind, beyond that painting.

Chapter Nineteen

Looking Back from Far Away

The good days grew fewer. Eric left, and Cornelia kept working on her book, and it sometimes seemed that without it she might have lost her hold on reality. The progress of the illness made itself felt more and more strongly.

When she was able, she wrote in the notebooks or talked into the tape machine. From day to day, they sent Amos into town to photocopy the manuscript and to send the work on to Lucius, for Cornelia never forgot that Emily had burned her mother's manuscripts.

Given any opportunity, she knew her aunt would do the same with hers. No explanation could persuade the woman that this was not a vicious attack upon herself. The fact that she was never once mentioned in its pages she would never have believed for a moment.

Jonathan came once a week, if not more often. From time to time, he brought his wife or his young daughter, and Cornelia enjoyed their visits, for too few new friends came into her life, now.

July wore away, and the weather turned hot. The air conditioners had to go on.

She hated losing the scents of the outdoors, the mown grass of the lawn, the scents of the four-o-clocks, the hay drying in the field beyond the lawn. She hated missing the calls of birds and the distant cattle lowing.

Closing the house seemed to shut her away from the world she would be leaving all too soon. Yet without the cooler air she could not breathe.

She did not, however, regret her approaching death. Her body was becoming unbearable, and even Jonathan's medications were working for shorter periods of time. He kept changing them, but never once did he cheat and give her something that would disorient her.

Pain, she found, was exhausting. Weariness, as much as illness, had her in its grip, and she found herself moving away from her body to a point at which nothing seemed real or important.

There came a day when she called Lucius. "Put the power of attorney into effect, Lucius," she said. "I am no longer able to cope with business. Stop forwarding the bills to me. Take care of everything. And keep tight control over the estate. When I go, my kin will move heaven and earth to get at the money.

"Don't let them. And never let anything upset the foundation for old dancers. I'm trusting you with that."

"I can hear it in your voice. You're worse. Cornelia, shall I come down there?" He sounded desperately sad.

"I would love to see you, but you would hate seeing me. I am so gross I can't bear to look into the mirror. Amanda combs my hair, so I won't have to. No, Lucius my friend, remember me as I was, as bad as that may seem, the last time you saw me. It is much worse now."

"I'll take care of things. Don't worry. And I love you, Cornelia Watson. You have been my true friend."

He had always been so dry and precise that his words astonished her. She knew, of course, that they loved each other with that rare, undemonstrative affection close friends sometimes find. She had never thought he would put it into words.

"I love you too, Lucius. Very much. Goodbye."

The conversation exhausted her. Amanda lowered the blinds, and Cornelia drifted into fitful sleep, lulled by the hum of the cooling system.

David waited there in her dreams, looking almost too well tailored, as usual. He seemed smug, and she felt about inside herself for the hurt and anger that always came with his memory. She tried to find the guilt she'd known at being conned.

Those feelings had run like hot springs beneath the cool discipline of her life, through all the years since she had sent him away. She'd avoided seeing him, thinking of him, even seeing people they both had known, in order to keep those feelings under control.

She found she had learned a lot since she last thought of him. She had faced and accepted death. She had glimpsed what might have been, and she found to her astonishment that nothing ran down those conduits of her heart where there had been so much bitterness. Not even the dust of an emotion was left within her. There was nothing stronger than a distant amusement.

"How young I was," she said, in that dream.

"Not all that young," came the comment deep inside her. "You were old enough, disciplined enough to recognize it for blind infatuation. Any but a fool would have seen through him, but you were wanting things you had put behind you. You had daydreams...."

Yes. It had been a daydream, a game she played with herself. David had been her pawn, she realized suddenly, rather than her being his.

She smiled in her sleep. The money she allowed him to take had been well spent, for he had satisfied a need, although he would never understand its nonphysical nature. He was used, poor man, to sexually frustrated women who wanted his body. He had never comprehended the fact that she would not spare the energy for that kind of relationship with him.

His company, his conversation had been enough for her game. She had been lucky to have the years of iron control behind her; if she had become physically involved it might well have destroyed her, emotionally. For Cornelia had known always that if she loved someone it would become the focus of her life. No life can have two centers, and she refused to allow her dancing to come second to anything.

That would have killed her as surely as her present illness was doing. Probably such a death would have been the more painful.

Something rippled the edge of her dream. She moaned softly, feeling the cool sheet, the light blanket that was necessary with the air conditioning. Was someone there? She opened her eyes.

Voices waked her. Amanda's, controlled but angry. A shriller voice, along with still a third, all too familiar. "You will not bother Cornelia. I won't have it. She has more than enough problems without the two of you pulling something. You aren't fit to polish her shoes!"

"We've called the sheriff. He's sending a deputy out, right now. You and those two Conwells are stealing my sister blind. We haven't heard from her in weeks, and we're worried. We insist on seeing her. She may even be dead. You could sit out here and draw her money without anyone knowing the difference."

Oh, my God! thought Cornelia. She forced herself to call, her voice rasping hoarsely. "Amanda, let them in. I'm awake. Now I'm awake."

There came a startled hush. Then Coral's heels tapped along the hall, followed by Emily's heavy tread.

"You sure you want to bother with them?" asked Amanda. She looked ready to pitch them both out with her own hands.

"Quite sure. You go wait with Amos and Ella. I won't need help, this time. I understand many things I never knew and I am something I never was before. Thank you."

Coral entered the room. She was flushed, and her step was hesitant. Emily was sallow, as usual, and she went to the recliner and pushed herself back comfortably. Coral perched on the edge of the rocker, looking nervous.

"Let me guess," said Cornelia, her voice a wheeze in her throat. "You've decided that I'm now so sick I can't run my own business. You've applied for custody and want to put me into a hospital. Take charge of all the property. True?"

Coral's eyes widened. "Just for your own good! You're too ill to know you're being robbed. Those people are using you!"

"And you resent having anyone else except the two of you using me." Cornelia managed a laugh.

They were so trivial. What had either ever done that made any difference? Neither had children. Neither had ever done a lick of useful work. It was sad. And they thought taking her money would make them important.

"Let me tell you a story," said Cornelia, "about a young woman with a strong and determined sister. A sister who made her feel inferior, because instead of digging in her heels and being someone useful, this young woman settled back and didn't do a thing. She was afraid of failing.

"She didn't marry." Coral looked relieved, for this couldn't be aimed at her.

"She didn't risk having children or train herself for any kind of work. She bullyragged her sister, though that busy person was too kind to mention it. When the sister died, the other took over her family, bullyragging her entire brood of children and her sick husband."

Emily thumped the recliner upright. "I took over my sister's orphans! Who else was there to do it?"

"Their father, a kind and competent man."

"Impractical as they come! Full of nonsense, singing in the fields, playing games when he ought to have been sweating or working for the church! He filled your heads with nonsense about books and music and things—like dancing!"

"Did he?" Cornelia saw Emily's pale skin darken with color. "What about my mother, who wanted to dance so desperately?"

Her aunt said nothing.

Cornelia went on, "This woman grew older. One of her nieces was much like her sister. The other was much like herself. She decided she must shape this one into a proper lady, full of all the ridiculous rules she'd been taught as a child. She turned her into an enemy of her own sister." She regarded them from a distance, too tired to be bothered with such silliness. But it was her burden, and she must carry it to the end.

"But no more. I understand now what happened to Coral. She was never strong enough to resist your stamp. I bear her no grudge, though I wouldn't let her manage a mockingbird. I am not even your enemy, Emily. You can't help being self-centered, any more than I can help being hard-headed. But that doesn't mean you can run over me, even now on my death bed.

"What you have done you will have to undo. I have given a power of attorney to my attorney, Lucius Amesbury, who is also my long-time friend. He is administrator of my will, and he is taking care of my business. Everything goes to Lisa in the will, as you very well know."

"That woman in there—she isn't in your will?" Emily looked gleeful.

"I gave Amanda fifty thousand dollars ten years ago. She invested it. I could not have bought the sort of care and affection she has given me, and I wanted her to be comfortable in her old age.

"I would have done the same for Coral, but she assured me she needs nothing. You, I know very well, are far more affluent than I am. You need nothing."

Emily turned scarlet, but she knew when she was outgunned.

"The deputy will be here with a warrant, almost any time now." Coral sounded worried. She hated looking like a fool.

Cornelia lifted the phone and dialed Lucius's number. The secretary answered at once.

"This is Cornelia Watson. I have an emergency, and I need to speak to Lucius."

"He's in conf...who did you say you are?"

"Cornelia Watson. It's important."

"Right away."

In seconds, Lucius was on the wire. "Cornelia, what's wrong?"

"A warrant committing me to the custody of my sister, who will put me into a hospital."

"Hang up. I'll burn the wires, fixing that."

She smiled at her kinfolk. "I suspect Sheriff Dobbs is getting a call, just about now. I am tired. Go home. Don't come back. I am not angry. I am no longer bitter, thank God. I am just sick to death of both of you."

They left quietly. The deputy must have been recalled, or they met him on the road, for he never arrived at all.

CHAPTER TWENTY

ESCAPE UP A LANE

Days slipped past, each one wearier than the last. Cornelia had all but finished the notebooks and the tapes. What she had not said she did not intend to reveal.

She had read her mother's books, finding them filled with strong characters doing extraordinary things. If she had guessed at the content of her mother's fiction she would have known that would be the sort of thing she would write.

August dried the world outside to crisp tan, and Amos muttered about the need for rain. It was so hot that even with the air conditioning the house sometimes grew too warm for comfort.

Cornelia had learned by necessity to pull out of her body, to shut away that bloated thing behind a door inside her mind. Beyond that doorway, she could almost become free.

The paintings gave her a goal. She lay for hours, studying the byways. She explored roads in France, lying beside streams running beneath Roman bridges or walking between pollarded trees, finding people and places, families and friends among the imaginary landscapes beyond the bends of the ways.

She wandered up streets in Paris that she had never had the time to explore. She learned much, in those internal journeys, that she did not commit to paper. More and more, she retreated into the painted worlds.

Her sister and her aunt did not return. She knew that Eric, when informed of their maneuver, had taken them in

138

hand, and the failure of their conspiracy seemed to split the two up, at least temporarily.

Without her brother to bring her out of her daydreams, Cornelia drifted through the days. The medication was strong enough to make it easy, and only Jonathan's visits brought her fully into the present of her physical condition.

"Am I being silly, wandering up and down roads that exist only on canvas and in my mind?" she asked the doctor, one day. "Is it rank escapism to leave this rotting hulk behind me and go free, without first paying the price of dying?"

Jonathan leaned back in the rocker and laughed. "Cornelia, when they passed out Puritan consciences, you must have gone through the line twice!" He leaned forward, hands clasped between his knees.

"I have patients in far better shape than you who have been sedated out of their minds for months. They don't want to know what's happening. Every time I let them come back, even just a bit, they beg to be put under again. Their bodies aren't dead—not quite—but they have been gone for a long time."

He looked into her eyes. "But here you are, alert and in command, learning every step of the way. If you can escape from your problem through imagination, have at it. I wish you could give me the recipe to pass on to others. Silly? I think it's wonderful!"

He rose and went to the window. Cornelia thought he seemed disturbed, but when he came back to her bedside there was no sign of it.

"In the early days of medicine, when anesthesia was invented, there were a lot of people, doctors as well as preachers, who were horrified at the idea of keeping people from experiencing pain. They said, with considerable backing from the churches, that man was born to suffering. Through dealing with pain, he learned and was purified."

He touched the rocker and made it move under his hand. "I wouldn't go quite so far, but I have known a few who refused painkillers all the way through. Those who survived are very different from the people they were before. Stronger. More self reliant and kinder."

He lit his pipe, and for a moment he drew on it. Cornelia waited, for she knew he was trying to tell her something important.

"The people I have known who died conscious, understanding what they faced, have not always been ones I admire. But even the worst have seemed more admirable to me, at the end, than those who want to be zonked out of their minds.

"Even bad old boys who spent their lives stomping all over society at large earned a bit of respect when they faced the end without flinching. Courage is a virtue, whatever our wimpish culture has to say about it."

"So it's somehow virtuous to go through the pain and the fear without trying to avoid it?" Cornelia shook her head. "This is just another sort of drug, you know. A non-physical one, but I, too, am trying to keep from feeling what is happening."

"No you're not. Each time you tell me about a trip into a painting, you seem more in control than before. More solidly planted inside yourself, determined to see this through in style. You have dropped all the tensions I could see in your eyes, when I first met you, did you know that?

"No, Cornelia, keep imagining your excursions. You are growing, from week to week. I can see it, if you can't."

He looked at his watch. "Oh, damn! I have to get back. Laurel has a piano recital at two-thirty. I promised to be there, if it was possible. She's good, you know." He quirked a brow at Cornelia.

She smiled. "I suspect she is. I have talked with her at length, Jonathan, while you consume Ella's dainties. She has drive. If music is her thing, encourage her. Thank heaven times have changed since I was young!'

He patted her shoulder. "I've wondered, Cornelia. If you hadn't had opposition from your aunt, would you have built up the head of steam that carried you right to the top of your field? Would you have been so utterly determined? Didn't that give you additional drive?"

Then he was gone, leaving her to think over what he'd said. It might well be true.

A ROAD OF STARS, BY ARDATH MAYHAR

She shifted her pillows and gazed at the painting Amanda had hung that morning. An English lane ran between a stone wall on the left and a low hedgerow on the right. It curved to reveal a humpbacked stone bridge over a shadowy stream. Beyond was a beech wood, huge, ancient, and beckoning.

"I have never stood in a beech wood," Cornelia said. "But I know how it must be. Someone told me, long ago." Then she was running lightly between wall and hedge, over the bridge, which was the very kind the Billygoats Gruff must have crossed to disturb the troll beneath it. She laughed. She feared no trolls, for her death waited for her in the flesh she had once again abandoned.

The stream chattered over pebbles, the sound following her as she approached the tremendous trees. Beneath the canopy of leaves there was a feel of antiquity so heavy that she paused, almost afraid. Then she heard music, gay dancing notes from a stringed instrument, perhaps a guitar. The path was plain. Ferns grew on either side, and bluebells could be glimpsed in a glade, catching a sprinkle of sunlight. But it was the music that pulled her forward until the forest closed behind her.

Someone was delighting in that melody, which caught her throat with delight and made her feet dance. She looked down to find that she wore light slippers and a full-skirted dress printed in rosebuds. She lifted the skirts in both hands and whirled with joy. Her feet followed the patterns of the music, jogging and waltzing and spinning down the path toward the musician. She danced around a bend and paused.

Sitting on a stone, which was a fellow to others standing in a semicircle behind him, was a bright-haired young fellow bent over his instrument, concentrating. As his fingers flew, the notes sang through the wood. She could see him smile as he played.

Cornelia imagined all the birds and hares and creatures among the trees and in the burrows beneath them dancing, too, as she had done. Again, she lifted her skirts and followed the notes of the waltz into which he had drifted.

When she was within arm's reach, she paused. "Hello," she said.

141

He looked up. The merriest blue eyes she had ever seen greeted her, though his fingers never missed a note. "You're not Pan," she said. "He would be more frightening, and besides he plays a syrinx. Are you the Pied Piper? With a guitar instead of a pipe?"

He laughed. "One of his direct descendants, I suspect. I practice out here, for my great-aunt hates music. As I play for my living, I can't stop just to placate her."

Cornelia perched beside him on the stone. "Aunts are like that. Mine didn't want me to dance; not at all. And that was what I was born to do. Why is that, do you suppose?"

"Oh, we're changelings," he said. Now his fingers picked out a wonderful theme, reminiscent of folk songs she had heard while touring Britain. "We can't blame the human folk for finding us difficult and disturbing.

"We are just...different. That's all; don't let it worry you."

The theme hummed beneath his fingers, filling the wood with rhythm. Cornelia watched as a butterfly came dancing down a ray of light, spun about his head, and flew away into the shadowy wood. The music rounded into a repetitive theme that grew fainter until it died away entirely.

"I'm Theron," he said. "And you?"

"Cornelia," she said, extending her hand.

They shook gravely. Then they rose, and Cornelia stared about. "Is this a megalithic circle, like those I've read about? It seems very small, but the stones are shaped just right."

"It is," he said. "This one began my love of the old places. I used to come here as a child and lie on this fallen stone and dream of those who raised it and the rest of its brothers. Who were they? What rites did they perform here?" He sighed wistfully. "Though my profession is very different, I have pursued that old interest, when I could."

He grinned. "I have stood upon the sites of almost every stone circle between Stenness, in the Orkneys, and the Trippet Stones in Cornwall. I have played my oldest musics there.

"I have watched the sun rise over Callanish in the Outer Hebrides, and I have played in the rain among the worn stumps of Scorhill on Dartmoor, which horses will not cross.

142

This world is older and stranger, Cornelia, than those who live here believe."

"And Stonehenge?" she asked.

He shrugged. "That baffles me. Too many have met there for too many purposes, over the ages. They have muddled the feel of it. And the phony druids sicken me." He frowned as he said that, but now the wrinkles smoothed from his forehead. He tossed back his long blond hair and reached for her hand.

"I shall show you the stones. They are not many and their ring is not large, but they are fascinating, nevertheless. Come!"

She followed as he stepped into the space between the menhirs. "See the cup marks?" he asked, pointing to the depressions cut into the stones. "Such a lot of hard work that must have been. I would give much to understand, truly understand, what went on here, three thousand years ago."

She looked up. "Have you tried going back? In your mind? As I am doing now?"

He stared, his eyes widening. "As you are now?"

"Actually, I am a middle-aged dancer, dying very slowly back in Texas. I came here through a painting, in my imagination and on purpose, because I wanted to see what was over the bridge. You could surely do that, couldn't you?"

With those words, she felt herself fading from his world. Theron reached for her hand, but his fingers slipped through hers without touching them. He looked sad, but she smiled at him.

"I loved your music!" she called, just before he and the wood and the stones thinned to nothing, and she found herself staring across the foot of the bed at the painting. She sighed. What a lovely dream that had been.

And Theron—she had no doubt he was real, someplace in England, playing his guitar and standing in stone circles.

Amanda came to the door. "You've been away," she said. "I can tell. Wish I'd been able to do that. I'd have seen the Pyramids, by now."

"Do you suppose I am a changeling?" Cornelia asked. "I was just told that by someone who might know."

"Wouldn't surprise me a mite," Amanda replied. "But I'd wonder what sort of creature changed you!"

Chapter Twenty-One

A Surge of Adrenalin

The world outside Cornelia's sickroom had receded from her mind. When the heat demanded that they turn on the air conditioner, it had seemed to shut her away from the country beyond the ash tree as nothing else managed to do. She wandered among her paintings, finding much to interest her, though she had not gone again as deeply as she had into that last. She recalled Theron with pleasure, for he had been such a happy person that his joy reverberated, still, inside her.

There came a day in late August, however, when the outside world intruded upon her again, vigorously and undeniably. Once she realized what was coming, a new surge of life seemed to fill her, for she had always been strongly affected by the weather.

Amanda began the day with a report gleaned from television. "Hurricane out in the Gulf is coming this way," she announced, as she opened the curtains and helped Cornelia wash up. "Should have known this place would come complete with storms!"

Cornelia shrugged beneath the washcloth. "They never get here as more than a bit of grungy weather. Lots of rain, gusts of wind, but nothing spectacular. I never remember one that made any big mess up here, after it left the Gulf. Don't let it worry you."

Amanda tweaked the sheets straight and changed the pillowcase. "I'm not worried. I like weather that puts its back into what it's doing. The TV people are all a-twitter, though."

Cornelia watched the sky all morning, studying the part she could see through the leaves of the ash tree outside. It was clouding up, more and more thickly. At last, she asked Amanda what was new on the storm.

"Came ashore at noon. Not too bad down there, but they say it's headed directly for us. Wind gusts up to sixty miles an hour. It'll probably lose a lot of punch as it comes, if it comes at all," she replied.

That night, there were no stars. The sky was one vast cauldron of heavy cloud. Cornelia felt in her bones the familiar excitement she always derived from violent weather. A tingle filled her bones...she understood why colts ran wildly through their pastures just before thunderstorms. She would have liked to do the same.

The wind began gusting lightly before dawn. By daylight, Cornelia was demanding to be helped into her chair. This would probably be her last storm, and she didn't intend to miss a minute of it.

Nothing happened for hours except light showers and nervous winds that switched direction from minute to minute. Yet that tingle still ran through her veins. She would have liked to go out onto the lawn and spin and leap and run with the last-year's leaves, caught up in the woods and sent flying.

Noon found things picking up. Cornelia hadn't thought much about her illness since the evening before, and now she forgot it entirely.

Something was going to happen. She felt it through herself, deep in bones and nerves. Something she had never seen—a good sendoff from the Weatherman!

The wind hit like a solid mass, thudding into the stout cypress walls with an impact that set the old house to complaining all through its timbers. It stood solidly, for it had withstood worse things than this. The shrubs outside Cornelia's window bowed low. Leaves and twigs scurried through the air, and something whipped flatly against the house.

"Take me out to the front," Cornelia said to her companion. "I want to see it head-on."

146

"With all that glass? Besides, Amos put up ply board over the big windows. Nothing's left to look out through but the ones with metal grillwork over them."

"Then I'll look from those. Hurry, Amanda! I don't want to miss a thing!"

Through the narrow windows' metalwork, she stared directly into the wind, which was slashing rain so hard it was running up the glass. A big branch sailed past and crashed into the side of the house, and the noise of wind and rain was so intense it reached a point at which the ears no longer registered the sound.

The forest she could see beyond the yard fence was laid over away from the wind, trembling and shaking from the pelting water. Even as she watched, a big oak beside the road snapped halfway up its trunk, and the heavy-leaved top sagged over onto the fence.

The wind grew stronger. Cornelia felt breathless, as the chaos outside grew more violent. Trees were turning over, their roots coming up out of the sodden ground. The ironwork outside her window was plastered with leaves so that she could hardly see out, now. There came a shock that shook the old house to its foundations.

Amanda caught the chair and turned it briskly toward the hall. "Enough is enough," she said. "You can watch from the leeward side, if you've got to. First thing you know, you're going to have a tree in your lap. With all the rest of your problems, having broken bones wouldn't be a bit of help."

Cornelia laughed. She felt young, excited, exhilarated, alive. The surge of adrenalin the storm had given her was pouring through her body, washing away, for the time being, the residue of illness.

Amanda put her into her bed and pulled back the draperies fully from her windows.

The sky was black, now, and thunder crashed toward them like the steps of a striding giant. Lightning stabbed downward, seeming to strike inside the room with them, and in its glare, Amanda looked out.

"Watch from here. Lord Almighty, it's just about in here with you, as it is. Look at that!" The older woman gasped and sank into the little rocker, reaching for Cornelia's hand.

Over the treetops, dancing along like some manic toy, moved a tornado's funnel. Lightnings ran up and down it; from time to time it threatened to dip into the forest, but always it lifted its delicate toe before touching down. It came from the southwest, diagonally toward the northeast. The house was almost directly on the line it seemed to be following.

"Go into the bathroom," said Cornelia. "Get into the bathtub and pull towels over you. Now, Amanda!"

"Here, let me get you back into your chair...."

"There's no time! Go! I'd just as soon dance with a tornado as with the thing I've been waltzing with all year. Scoot!"

With reluctance...but with speed...Amanda left, closing the door behind her.

Cornelia turned so she could see from the window on that side of her bed. Something was knocking hard at the walls of her chest, and she realized it was her heart. It, at least, had sense enough to be afraid.

She was not. That elemental thing that was dipping and swaying and groping toward her amid flashes and rumblings was only death and destruction. She held within her own body the match for it.

"What could you possibly do to me that hasn't been done already?" she called aloud.

Then she laughed, high and long. She had not felt such exaltation in years. The long rope of funnel dipped deeply into the trees. Debris fanned out from it in a dark cloud, black on black, before it pulled up again, gracefully, leisurely, and moved above the house and the wood beyond it, she saw as she turned quickly to watch from the window on that side.

"Damn! It missed me!" she said.

Only when it was gone did the rain's thunder impinge on her senses. She could hear a drip somewhere in the room. She suspected there would have to be roofing done on the house as soon as they could manage it. A wind like the one they were having played havoc with tin and shingles alike.

The worst of the wind was dying away, now, though the rain continued as if the hurricane had been a sponge soaking up the Gulf waters, now being squeezed out over the land. She sighed and lay back, letting the pounding of the rain lull her nerves. Light slowly returned to the sodden world outside.

"That was worth living to see," she said to Amanda, as the old woman crept back into the room.

"It's over?"

"The worst of it. You missed it...that was something! The funnel came right over us. Touched down over in the woods toward Farthing's hayfields and zoomed along for a bit. Then it looped up and hopped right over us. Missed us entirely.

"That would have been some classy way to go, carried away by a tornado. Can't you see the headlines? 'DYING DANCER DISAPPEARS IN CYCLONE!'"

Amanda sank again into the rocker and drew a deep breath. Then she began to laugh. The rocker itself was quaking beneath her. "By God, Cornelia, I'm glad I hooked up with you. There's not but one, and if I'd missed you, it would have been a pity. You know why that tornado jumped over you? I can tell you! It was scared to tangle with you, that's why!"

Cornelia began to laugh. They whooped together so loudly that Amos and Ella came from their refuges in pantry and hall to see what was happening.

"Just a slight case of hysteria," hiccupped Amanda. "Everything all right, Amos?"

"A couple of windows are shattered, but I put up boards so the rain can't ruin anything. We'll fix 'em tomorrow," he said.

"Lights are out, of course, but Ella's got the kerosene lamps ready to light, when it gets dark." He glanced out at the afternoon, which was by now almost indistinguishable from night. "Darker," he amended.

"Why not light them now?" asked Cornelia. "We'll all sit around in the kitchen and roast marshmallows over the chimneys. We used to do that when I was a child, when the lights went out. That happened pretty often, and Eric and I used to look forward to it as if it was a treat. And of course it was. Mom made anything at all into a treat."

Amanda helped her into the chair again, and the three trundled into the kitchen, where Ella had already lighted four big kerosene lamps. Their mellow glow seemed appropriate in the big old-fashioned kitchen.

It winked from the china in the cabinet and the brass plates hung on the walls. It made mirrors of the windows, and Cornelia glanced, now and again, toward the glass to see the four of them sitting around the table, each toasting a marshmallow over a lamp chimney.

Now and then a sugary drip went into the lamps, but it didn't bother them. If they spent the next day cleaning up, that was fine, too. Now they felt like children, freed from care. They giggled, as Amanda brought out a packet of Graham crackers, and they put the hot, sticky melts onto the crackers and made sandwiches.

They ate until they felt stuffed. Cornelia had had little appetite for weeks, but this was special, and she ate greedily. They smiled at each other until their eyes grew heavy. Then Amanda took Cornelia away to her bathroom to remove some of the debris.

"I feel like a survivor of the *Titanic*," said Amanda, as she turned on the water, blessing the storage tank and the gas hot water heater.

"Did you ever see a house that had been hit by a tornado?" asked Cornelia, holding onto the rod in the shower, as the warm water poured gratefully over her.

"Not as I recall."

"You'd really feel like a survivor of the *Titanic*, if that thing had hit us. If, that is, you survived at all. A house will just...just go away. The roof flies off. The walls come apart and are blown away. I've seen nothing left but a floor and a woods-full of tin and timber."

She hung onto Amanda's shoulder while they made their way to her bed. She sat, swung up her legs with less difficulty than usual, and lay back. Then she closed her eyes and sighed.

"This has been one more day!"

"You'll pay for it tomorrow. All that energy—it had to come from somewhere. But I must say that when your East Texas decides to put on a show, it's worth the price of admission," Amanda said. "You want to read a while?"

"Yes. Just leave this lamp. I'll blow it out, when I'm done. The lights will probably be back on in a day or two. Good night, Amanda."

Cornelia lay quietly, watching the lamplight flicker on the old furniture, the books, the windows. Lightning still flashed outside, from time to time. The rain was still such a constant roar on the roof that it became almost inaudible from sheer familiarity. In the distance, a dull rumble of thunder muttered to itself in the wake of the worst of the storm. A sort of farewell, Cornelia thought.

The painting on the wall facing her bed was a *mélange* of reflections, as the lamplight bounced off the strongly brushed oil. It was as intriguing as a mystery as it had been as a landscape.

She blew out the lamp and lay in the darkness, reliving the storm. Oh it had, indeed, been worth living to see!

Chapter Twenty-Two

Among the Shaggy Mountains

Eric came to check on their welfare, bringing new roofing and window glass. Jonathan paid a flying visit, after delivering every baby that had been due for the next few weeks. Then Cornelia sank into her lethargic state again, and Amanda hung a painting of a highway through the mountains.

Cornelia slipped into a doze as she gazed at it. The highway, a strip of silver, curved away between two mountains, disappearing into a forested canyon, and she felt she must follow...

She was driving around a curve. On her left was a thin silver ribbon of river, and on the right a mountaintop loomed into the clouds. Ahead was a solid wall of ridges, shaggy with fir trees. The road looped abruptly around the ankles of one soaring ridge, went over the instep of another, and entered a long canyon. She drove across a bridge to find herself in the main street of a tiny town, which had been hidden in its cupped valley.

One side held homes, bright with flower beds and climbing vines. The other was shop fronts, each a different color and sporting neat signs.

She turned into a space in front of a restaurant, whose front window was a billow of spotless white curtains, setting off copperware and a huge philodendron. A wide-hipped blonde met her at the door and ushered her to a table.

The place was neat. A Dutch clock tocked on the wall, its pear-shaped weights catching the light. A girl in a lace apron came with silverware.

"Would you like tea?"

"I'd love some." She studied the menu carefully. "And the soup with brown bread, then the trout." She was suddenly ravenous.

"Have you visited Canada before?" the girl asked, as she took the menu. "Do you like unusual places to stay?"

Cornelia nodded. "I do, indeed, though I haven't visited Canada except for brief appearances in the cities."

"There is a place outside town you might like, to the north. Where the highway turns away to the west, Alfred's inn sits in its own little valley. Tell Alfred Susan sent you."

After her meal, Cornelia followed the highway north and then west and found the sign:

ALFRED'S MOUNTAIN VIEW INN

There was absolutely nothing to see but mountains, which thrust tree-furred toes from all sides. The tiny valley was cupped entirely by the shaggy heights.

Cornelia admired the red tile roofs of the cottages clustered about a brick office. Flowering shrubs lifted bouquets of lavender and pink and rose on branching arms. She felt herself relaxing, as she pulled up and stopped. A man as wide as the hostess at the restaurant came out, exuding welcome from every pore.

"I need a cottage for the night. Susan sent me, back there at the restaurant in town," she told him.

"I'll put you in the cottage at the back, beside the trail up into the forest. A good clear track, that is, and nobody has ever been lost following it to the top of the mountain." He helped her put her case into the neat cottage, and left her to her own devices.

She was settled before the sun went too far down the west, and although there was cloud cover, there was still a bright silver spot where the sun rode high. She had time for a walk, before dark.

Changing into jeans and boots, she tucked her small camera into the pocket of her windbreaker and tied the jacket around her waist by the sleeves. Then she went out and stood staring up at the mountain.

It was like being in the bottom of a green bowl. The mountains were like great loaves set on end, and the firs that had seemed to be bushes, in the distance, now were great trees with butts six or eight feet in diameter.

She found the path easily, beginning on the pebbled area joining the paths about the cottages. A fence at the back was spanned by a stile, and she crossed it onto a path covered with shredded bark. That was evidently well used, for the track was trodden flat.

She looked closely to find deer tracks in the loose dirt at its edge; birds' three-toed prints joined the tiny paw prints of chipmunks. She breathed deeply, feeling the clean scent of the trees penetrate to the bottoms of her miraculously clear lungs. Vigor filled her.

Her dancer's muscles carried her up the steep path, and as she went up she found the trees even larger than those below. The track wandered back and forth in loops, anchoring upon boulders and wandering over the roots of the firs. She went forward, wanting to see the view that must be visible from the height above her.

She slowed, after a time, for her wind, at this elevation, was not quite sufficient for her needs. She let her racing heart catch up as she leaned against a rough tree trunk, watching the path behind her. Something was moving back there, following her, she thought.

A furry face peered over a stony shelf. Bright eyes watched her speculatively. Other hikers must have fed the little beast, and she hated to disappoint it. Was there anything in her pocket that might serve?

She felt about. Camera in the right pocket. Aha! Crackers in the left, with three left in the packet.

She took the crackers out and broke them to bits, moving quietly toward the spot where the chipmunk waited. She laid a line of crumbs along the stone slab and then stepped back to watch. Around her, the forest was quiet except for the rustle of firs in the breeze.

154

After a few minutes, the eyes glinted again. The head came up, and a plump body skittered onto the shelf, darting toward the food. Another chipmunk followed the first. They tucked cracker crumbs into their cheeks, swelling them into mumpish lumps. They scurried back into hiding, came back for more, and Cornelia watched with delight. When they had finished the line of crumbs, she sighed with satisfaction, starting up the slope again. The sun was lower, and she did want to see the view.

When she broke out of the trees on top of the mountain, she was in a saucer of stone, set at an angle in the curve of grass ending the path. The slope toward the west was treeless, bright with fireweed.

She looked across another valley, where mist caught the light of the veiled sun. The vista seemed draped in layers of chiffon, and small canyons rayed out from the valley's bowl, each filled with shadow.

From overhead there came a shriek. An eagle? The wind, which had been light, now picked up velocity, tearing away the veils of mist and pushing aside the clouds. The sun came through, lighting the vapors to gold.

Leaves of birches glittered along the distant streams. The bark of the few firs on the peak turned red. Cornelia's hair blew back from her face as she turned into the gusts, longing to take off from that perch and fly down the long reaches into the valley.

She felt strong enough to deal with anything that might ever happen to her. The lightness and freedom holding her went deeper than her body, extending into the depths of her mind and her spirit.

The sun was going down, now, and she knew she must go back, but she sighed with satisfaction. It had been a wonderful day. Why had she never taken the time to do such things, defying her iron schedule and her demanding work?

She turned—and she was again in her room, looking up at the gargoyle atop the Monster Bed. She had not done them because there was no time. No energy. And yet if she had taken the time, expended the energy, perhaps her work would have been better, still, for the experience.

Yet she had known that day, if only in dream. She had fed the chipmunks, climbed the mountain and looked down from the top. She had breathed the clean air of high places.

Amanda came in softly and asked, "You awake?"

"Yes. I went up there." She gestured toward the painting. "It was wonderful, full of things I never knew before. It washed away the weariness, Amanda. Every time I go into a painting, I seem to learn something valuable."

"You need food," Amanda said.

"I ate in a tiny restaurant in a town hidden in the mountains. It had a Dutch clock on the wall."

"You're light-headed! People don't dream Dutch clocks!" Amanda bustled toward the kitchen.

Cornelia yawned. The journey had helped her. She reached for the phone and touched the buttons. It was past five in New York, but she knew Lucius often worked late. He sounded worried when he heard her voice. "Cornelia! How are you feeling?"

"Not too bad," she said. "Dying is very educational, did you know that? Nobody ever told me it would be. I wonder how many people suspect it to be true."

His laugh had a touch of hysteria. "You are totally insane, Cornelia. I never heard it said, rumored, or hypothesized that death could be a learning experience."

"It is, believe me. I'm learning not to be angry about anything. Not to worry. Not to cling to matters that have become irrelevant. It is very interesting." She paused to let her heart ease. "It won't be very long, now. I don't object in the slightest. I just wanted to hear your voice again and to tell you...."

"What?"

"That if things had been different, I might have set my cap for you, when Janet died."

He chuckled. "I wouldn't have run very fast. You could have caught me easily."

"I know. Goodbye, Lucius. Take care of yourself."

He didn't answer, and she knew it was because he could not. She heard his receiver click down.

"Now I've made Lucius sad," she said aloud. "Dammit!" But she wasn't sorry to have spoken to him one last time. He had been, next to Amanda, her best friend. With Eric, the three of them had comforted her Spartan life with human ears to listen and human hearts to care.

CHAPTER TWENTY-THREE

STONE BELLS

The days became harder. Her kidneys, which had been declining slowly, deteriorated more rapidly. The edema, already gross, became worse. She felt like a water balloon, ready to drop on some unsuspecting head and burst. Jonathan changed her medication, and for a time the new stuff helped, but they both knew she was failing. The end of the summer would see her own end, and the fall would see her ashes in place in the family cemetery. She didn't care.

Every breath came harder, and it became more difficult to lose herself in a painting. Several times, she failed to find her way into intriguing paths.

Eric came almost every day. She asked about his business affairs, but he shrugged. "That will wait," he said. "You won't. I'm going to be with you as long as I can. When you're gone, I will need all the piled up business to take my mind off things."

She was too weak to talk with him very much. She smiled, when she opened her eyes to find his furrowed face staring at her from the rocker. Breath was too hard-won to use much for conversation.

To her surprise, Raiford Pierce came again to see her. He seemed somewhat ill-at-ease when he settled into the rocker. "They tell me you are not doing well, Miss Watson. I wanted to let you know that you gave me a lot to think about, when I came before.

"I have thought about what you told me. I have looked at your tapes and read your notices. We country preachers

158

tend to become arrogant, you know, as if only we had access to God. We lose sight of things outside our own small world, and you reminded me of those. I believe I am a better man for knowing you."

She blinked with astonishment. "I'm no saint," she whispered. "Just learning to die. Almost there now, but I've discarded a lot of faults along the way."

"I don't know any saints," he replied. "I wouldn't know what to do with one. But I've known a few courageous people, and you are one. I have seen *Life of the Heart*, and as far as I can tell, knowing nothing about your art, you served God well with that. It spoke to my own heart. That's all anyone can do."

She was surprised that his eyes were full of tears. She reached feebly to take his hand, and he caught hers eagerly.

"If I've helped, I'm glad. Goodbye, Mr. Pierce."

He laid her hand carefully beside her. "Go with God," he said, and she was not offended, though she disliked religious sentiments, ordinarily.

After he went, she considered what he had said. She had not tried to convince him of anything. Strange.

She looked up at the new painting on the wall. A woman in a blue robe, barefoot in the dust of a jungle trail, was moving along it. Where was she going?

Cornelia had always been intrigued by the Far East. Now she wondered what was beyond the frond of foliage hiding the trail beyond the woman. She closed her eyes and felt dust beneath her feet.

A strange sound came from the jungle ahead. Not a gong, not a church bell, it had timbres of both. She went forward, pushing rubbery fronds out of her way. Ahead, she saw an old man tottering along, supporting himself on a crutch. She moved up beside him and put her shoulder under his arm.

He smiled, his toothless mouth forming words she could not understand. She smiled back and his wary look softened. They went on together, following the crooked path until they broke free of the jungle and stood in a clearing around a stone temple. Ornate cupolas decorated its round roof, and the clearing was studded with strange shapes. Huddles of robes seemed to have been discarded in untidy heaps about the clearing.

The old man freed himself gently and bowed his head. He moved toward one of the odd formations, and Cornelia followed. Those stones were large, half the size of an automobile. Rectangular, with curved sides, they looked like huge loaves of bread, but each of the corners was set upon a thick stone post.

She bent and looked beneath the nearest, the smallest of the lot. It was hollow, though the stone walls were thick. She stood and looked about at the other five, which ranged from this one to a huge stone near the farther edge near the jungle.

What could they be? She looked down at the hammer hanging from a cord. Its head was a sphere of gray stone, into which a black wooden handle was set. Even as she wondered, a sound shook her bones.

"TOOOOMM!"

The vibration seemed to move through her body, setting up resonances in nerves and flesh and bones. It quivered in her skull, shaking out any thought that might have lodged there. The quivering died, and she stepped forward to stare down the row.

The old man had a hammer in hand, swinging it toward the third of the stone bells. "TOOOOMMMMM!"

This was deeper, commanding, compelling. She shivered.

He made his way from bell to bell, striking a pattern of notes as he struck each stone. His lips moved, and she knew he was praying.

The effect of the sounds on her made her understand these bells to be very powerful, very sacred. They set up a field in which the mind and the spirit reached outward, away from the housing flesh.

She took up the hammer of the smallest bell and struck the stone lightly. "TOOM!"

Her mind lightened, as cares scattered like a swarm of flies, leaving her free. This bell affected those in the midst of life, relaxing the spirit. It calmed worries and damped fears. She smiled and moved to the next, which was larger.

"TOOOOM!"

160

Tension left her body. The last of bitterness and anger drained from her, leaving her clean and light.

She struck the third, harder than the last. That had the effect of some drugs she had taken, early in her illness. Her head spun, and she felt disoriented. Things took on different shapes and colors.

The old man ahead of her suddenly seemed to stand straighter.

A fourth bell brought another blow of a heavier hammer. This was the one her companion had struck first, but she was now prepared for its unsettling effect.

She stepped forward to see the old man striking the last of the stone bells, his feeble arm trembling with the effort. She thought for a moment she was seeing double. He went on beyond the bell, his stride free, his shoulders lifting and squaring. At the foot of the bell lay a crumpled shape dressed in his shabby robes, holding the crutch in one bony hand.

She bent over the still body. The skin was ashen, though the hand was still warm. He was quite dead, though his bright shadow walked away into the jungle.

She stared at the last pair of bells. So this was the way she might use to leave her life, if she wanted. She could strike the last bell and go free into whatever came next. It was a great temptation. The discomfort of the past days was strong in her mind, as she gazed at the stone hammer, the huge bell, and the waiting jungle, into which the old man had disappeared.

She struck the fifth bell.

"DDOOOOMMM!"

Her body lightened, her spirit loosened inside her. She could go free, here and now, without any more suffering.

She hurried to the last bell, took the hammer in hand. It was heavier than the others, the ball of stone forming its head as large as a cannonball.

She lifted it on its cord, swung it back, and began the forward motion. She was stopped by a voice, alien and yet strangely familiar.

"Not now," it said. "Not now. It is not your time. Go all the way, not just part of it. Learn all you can, while you have the chance. Then you may go free, without fear of return to the Wheel."

She paused, looking at the hammer. At the bell. Nobody was in sight.

"The pain is part of it?"

"Much of it. In a way, it may be all of it, for pain opens the way for understanding. That opens the path for enlightenment.

"Come to the light, Cornelia, but come at your own time. This is an unworthy short-cut. For him it is the right way. For you it would be wrong."

She let the hammer go back, very carefully, into position. She turned from the last bell, recognizing the voice. It was her own, unoccluded by fluid and pain. She had counseled herself through this temptation.

That told her something of the distance she had traveled along the road she must finish. In the beginning, if she had known the strange things she would learn in pursuing her own death, would she have come? She wondered. The jungle path was before her, and she pushed through the leaves into the suffocating scent of flowers. The dust was hot beneath her bare soles.

She walked along, wondering when she would return to her own body, her Monster Bed in her grandfather's house. The path wound on, through patches of sun and stretches of shadow.

A woman came to meet her, her face drawn and gray. Her skin was almost greenish, and she breathed with the terrible care that Cornelia had learned in the past months. They paused on the path, facing each other.

Cornelia smiled and held out a hand. The woman looked startled, but she began smiling. Her work-worn paw came out to meet Cornelia's.

"This is your path. That is your place. It is your fitting death you go to find," she said.

The woman looked at her wonderingly. She spoke, but Cornelia didn't understand her words. Yet she understood the meaning in them, the look of compassion in the dark eyes, and the squeeze of the hard hand.

They sighed together, and their hands parted. The woman went forward up the path, and Cornelia moved down it...into her own room, her own bed. The sun was down among the treetops, slanting rays lighting the bedspread, the rug, and the watercolor on the wall. The woman on the path looked very familiar.

Cornelia pushed herself up a bit and stared. It was the same one. She wished her well. That last bell would free her of the thing devouring her.

She turned as Amanda came into the room. "You've been gone again! It's not like normal sleep. More like some kind of trance. One of these days...." Her voice caught in her throat. "You're not coming back."

"When that happens," Cornelia croaked, "be glad, Amanda. Be happy for me. I almost escaped, this time.

"Something made me come back, for I haven't reached the end of my road, yet. There is still something to learn or to do before I go free into the jungle."

Chapter Twenty-Four

Letting Go

She woke to the sound of rain on the roof. The air conditioner was off, and the windows had been opened to let in the scent of wet woods and fields. She breathed more easily, remembering other, happier awakenings.

Now she had now gone past physical needs. It was time to get her emotional house in order, and she called Amanda. "Call my aunt and my sister," she said, her voice rasping with effort. "I must see them."

"But they upset you! You told them never to come back!" Amanda protested.

"That was before I had gone this far with my education. Please. Call them."

The morning passed slowly, and just before noon she heard the sound of a car in the drive.

Rain still misted down, cooling the soil, making beads of moisture inside each square of the window screen. She focused on those as she heard Emily's fat feet thudding up the hallway. Cornelia waited, eyes closed, as the two came into the room. She didn't move, for that had become almost impossible, now.

"Cornelia?" Coral sounded hesitant. Her voice was strangely gentle.

She opened her eyes. "I wanted to see you both. To apologize."

They stared at her, then at each other. Their expressions were identical ones of sheer astonishment. "For what?" That was Emily, sounding dazed.

164

"For being angry. For resenting you and feeling bitter all these years. For some of the things I have said. Although they were true, they were not kind."

Amanda touched her forehead with a damp cloth, as she struggled for breath.

Coral came close and took one of her hands. "Mr. Pierce talked to us, after he came to see you," she said. "He told us we were wrong about what you did, all those years. He showed us some things we'd never thought about. He was stern with us, and I was angry. But I went off and thought about what he said, and I knew he was right. Emily too."

Cornelia thought there were tears in Coral's eyes, and she certainly didn't want a sentiment-ridden baring of souls at this point. She wanted to clean house, not to get sloppy. "That is neither here nor there." She gasped and struggled to regain the rhythm of her breathing.

"What you think and do is your business. Do what you think fit about it. I let myself become bitter, and I was angry for years. That's corrosive and eats you away from inside."

Amanda wiped her face again and put the straw for ice water between her lips. She sipped and went on. "I have been guilty of that, and I'm sorry. I can't go until I make it clear nothing you said or did justified my allowing myself to be affected in that way." She gazed up at the two, trying for clarity. "I did what I wanted to do, and I did it well. I knew my chosen art was going to make problems with some of my family, down here in the Bible Belt, but I made the choice freely."

She saw a glance pass between Coral and Emily, but she went on, "I should have shut off my feelings at that point, let it pass over. I wasn't wise enough. It's only fair to tell you that if I had not loved you both you couldn't have hurt me. I couldn't quite close off my heart from you, even when I thought I hated you." She squeezed Coral's hand.

"Forgive me for my anger."

Emily's face was working, her lips pulling in and out and her forehead deeply grooved. "I knew all the time," she said, her voice husky. "I helped raise you, and I knew you. But I couldn't stand your going out and doing things I couldn't. Your mother was just the same." She fumbled for a handkerchief and blew her nose noisily.

"That's why I burned the papers. I didn't want my sister to do things I couldn't. I wanted her to be just like me, somebody without the courage to try things other people don't have the nerve to think of doing."

Coral was staring at her. "You mean you lied to me? You knew all the time?"

Emily nodded.

"You wicked old woman!"

Cornelia tugged at her sister's hand. "Here, don't go doing the same thing I did. I just told you it was foolish and self-destructive. Believe me, those feelings are harder on the one having them than on the one who's their object."

Coral bent and touched Cornelia's forehead. "We've wasted too many years! And I never saw you dance!"

"There are the tapes and the movies. The book will come out next spring, with a lot of photographs. It will be like one last visit with me."

"That book!" Emily straightened and blew her nose. "What did you say about the family?"

"Practically nothing. Not one word about any of our family problems, certainly. This is a book about my work, rather than my private life, and I think you may enjoy it. There is one thing I wonder, Emily. Why didn't you go out and find something you could do well and DO it?"

"I was afraid. Afraid I'd fail, and people would laugh at me."

Cornelia's heart gave a soggy heave. Her breath caught, and she felt the dull pain intensify. She loosed Coral's hand and pressed her own to her throat. Was this the end? She wasn't yet finished!

Amanda herded the two out of the room and was back at once. "It's all right. They understand. I think you're crazy, but you got through to them. They left looking more human than I've seen them, yet.

"Now you relax and quit trying to talk. Jonathan's on his way."

Cornelia couldn't speak, but her gaze demanded an answer.

166

Don't Overthink It.

"Oh, I called him when I called them. I knew you'd need him, however it went. He agreed. You just hold on, and he'll help you breathe better."

He did, just a bit. She could only smile as he came into her room.

After giving her the shot, he sat in the rocker, telling her about Laurel's recital. He was a soothing presence in the room, and she drifted in and out of focus, as the congestion began to ease.

He was still there when she slid into sleep. She rested well, dreamless in the night of the drug.

It was morning when she woke. Sun lighted the ash tree, making its leaves shine after the rain of the day before. Amanda moved about the room, closing the windows and turning on the air conditioner, for already it was growing hot.

"Steamy outside?" she asked.

"You could cook a tough chicken just by putting it on the porch," she said.

"I believe I could eat," Cornelia whispered. "Something easy."

While she waited for breakfast, Ella helped her bathe, and she felt almost human when she lay back against clean pillowcases, beneath crisp sheets. As she finished eating the bit she could manage, the phone rang in the hall, her bedside telephone being connected only for outgoing calls.

She sipped the last of the orange juice, and as she set aside the glass, Amanda came into the room.

"Well, just what we need. Another relative. That was Lisa, and she and her folks are coming out." Amanda looked sour.

A rush of weariness flooded through Cornelia. After yesterday, the last thing she needed was another emotional binge. But she could endure it; she knew that now. "Get out my nicest nightgown. And brush my hair, will you? Young people ought not to be depressed any more than we can help. Death can't be avoided, but untidiness can."

When the sound of Eric's car doors slamming came to her ears, she was neat and fairly rested. She knew she looked as well as possible, which was not wonderful but at least respectable. She ached for her brother, seeing her as she now was. He was suffering almost more than she was.

She glanced at the painting Amanda had hung for that day. A vista of slopes stretched away across forested ridges, framing a wagon track along which two young girls walked. They were dressed in their Sunday best, polished and shining. She smiled. Their dark faces were alight with pleasure. It was a quiet picture, but full of life.

Then her people were at the door, and as she looked up she felt a jolt of shock run through her. David was the first to enter her room.

Eric followed Lisa, and the three lined up at the foot of the bed, gazing at her. Even Eric, who had visited only two days before, seemed saddened at her appearance.

"You look like a hanging jury," she wheezed. "But it's too late; the death sentence has already been handed down." She realized, too late, that it was a cruel thing to say. Her wicked sense of humor had betrayed her before, but such things popped from her mouth at the most unsuitable moments.

Eric flinched. Lisa winced, but David seemed unaware of any problem. He was smiling down, and something in his face seemed nastily triumphant.

Lisa moved to kiss her aunt lightly on the forehead. When she straightened, Cornelia saw she looked softer, happier, more glowing than she had ever seen her niece before.

"You're in love," Cornelia said.

"I'm going to be married!" She moved to stand beside David, taking his hand and gazing up adoringly.

Cornelia felt her heart thud. A cold dismay filled her, as she thought of the meaning of this sudden situation.

"David and I wanted to tell you as soon as possible," Lisa said.

"I'll just bet he did," sneered the wicked voice inside her. But she kept the words behind her teeth as she smiled.

Chapter Twenty-Five

An Unimpeded View

Eric sensed something wrong. He glanced at David, back at Cornelia. She knew she'd concealed her surprise and dismay, but her long-held linkage with her brother warned him of something amiss.

"Well, David," she said, "I haven't seen you for years. You look well." She knew he was hearing her unspoken question: Why have you sought out my niece? As if I didn't suspect, already! And why have you brought her here?

Cornelia knew the answers, she thought, but, strangely, she felt neither angry nor hurt. She seemed to be a passenger on a train, watching a scene alongside the track that was receding rapidly from view. It had nothing to do with her, now, though she felt a responsibility toward her niece.

Lisa looked surprised. "You know each other?"

"We used to," Cornelia said. "Years ago." She glanced about for chairs. "Won't you all sit down? Eric, would you ask Amanda for another chair?"

With his usual intuition, Eric took Lisa with him, leaving his sister alone with David. She lay quietly, watching the man, waiting.

He still looked young—he was only in his mid-forties, after all, a month or so younger than she. He had never, so far as she knew, been ill in his life, and he made certain to keep fit. The features were still clean-cut, the lines about his pale eyes deeper, the smudges below them darker, perhaps, but not by much.

169

"So you decided to find a way to get your hands on my money, after all," she said. Her tone was amused, for that was so like him.

He looked disturbed. He had always, before this, possessed a handle on her emotions, he had thought. That was his talent: the ability to assess and to use other people's emotional loopholes.

It had puzzled and angered him that he had not been able to push her into a physical relationship, but she had always known that to be the last nail in the coffin of her independence.

Now she regarded him coolly. She saw a rather shopworn gigolo. High class, of course, well bred and well spoken, but without any talents except one, which seemed rather pitiable.

"You never did," she said.

"Did what?" His head went up, as if he scented danger.

"Use those connections you said you had made through me in order to make your own fortune. To become powerful and to use people. Too bad. You have so little." She stared demandingly into his pale eyes.

"How did you find Lisa? She was still a child in Texas when you knew me."

"You underestimate your gossip value, my dear Cornelia. I have kept up with you and yours, all the way. I knew when you became ill. I know the contents of your will, believe it or not. You have been generous with your niece, haven't you?"

She was not, somehow, surprised. "Lucius would never tell you anything, so somewhere among his employees is a typist who is either too young to be wise or old enough to be desperate. You pursued her until you found what you wanted. That's the way you operate.

"A shoddy method, but your very own." She laughed, genuinely amused, for the codicil concerning the trust for Lisa was separate from the main will.

He looked uncomfortable. He was not used to being taken lightly, for she had never done that. Even at the end of their friendship, when she saw through him to her own disgust, she had not laughed at him. She had been nearer, at that time, to weeping.

"I thought you'd be angry. You were rather upset when last we talked," he said.

"Oh, I used to be. I have been angry with many people for many reasons, over the years, but I have put that behind me. I can no longer afford anger or bitterness or fear.

"At this point I am on the interface between life and death, David. A time will come when you will stand where I am now. Unless you put some effort into mending yourself, you are going to find that a terribly hard thing to do. It could be terrifying, if you had nothing inside with which to deal with it."

There came a clatter in the hall, and Eric came in with a wicker chair from the sun porch. Lisa was talking with Amanda, as they approached behind him. Cornelia smiled, feeling serene and in control of things.

David's fair skin was flushed. He covered his discomfort by helping Eric place a chair so that Lisa could sit on one side of her aunt, while Eric occupied the rocker and David the recliner.

Lisa was being gracious to Amanda, which told Cornelia the extent of her happiness. She turned to take the girl's hand.

"So you have decided to marry David," she said. "I would like, later, to have a quiet talk with you about some matters, but for now I am just glad for you. How does your mother feel about it?"

"Mama is ecstatic. She can see that David is a real gentleman, not like the rednecks around here. He makes me feel special!"

"Oh, I believe that," her aunt murmured. "I have known David for years."

Eric's internal warning system was working at peak efficiency. He heard all the shading beneath Cornelia's innocent words. She saw him look closely at David.

Lisa squirmed in the wicker chair. "I need to ask you some things, Cornelia. While there's time. I don't really feel good about doing this, but it may be the only chance I get to talk to you about it. Do you mind? Lucius suggested it."

"About the inheritance? Of course. Would you rather do it privately? Eric could take David out and show him around the farm. He might be interested, as it will be yours rather soon, now."

David glanced at her sharply, as if wondering what she intended. He left gladly with Eric, leaving the two alone.

Cornelia said, "What is it that you want to know? Everything, I thought, was quite clear in the letter I gave you."

Lisa looked uncomfortable. "But David doesn't know everything is in trust. He thinks it will all come to me at once.

"I didn't exactly tell him a fib—he knew a lot about the will and he just assumed it was all there was. I never told him differently, because I'm afraid it may upset him, when he finds out. Can you change things, so I can have everything without its being in trust? I know that was intended to protect me, but now I have David to care for my interests."

"Do you believe David might back off, if he knew about the trust?" Cornelia asked.

Lisa looked shocked. "Oh, no! He isn't after the money—he really loves me. He shows it so clearly! I just want to give him everything I can."

Cornelia closed her eyes. This was going to be tricky, requiring a delicate touch and a lot of tact.

"I'm getting tired," she told Lisa. "Go out and join your father and David. Let me rest, while you have lunch, and then come and talk with me again. When I have looked into things, I will decide what to do."

Looking slightly disappointed, Lisa rose. "All right. Oh, Aunt Cornelia, I am so happy. I don't want anything to go wrong!"

Cornelia ached for the girl. She had chosen a doomed course, and she could not see that it could only end in disaster, now or later. Through no fault of her own, Lisa had become entangled in nets woven when she was a child.

If Cornelia had still possessed the ability to become angry, she would have been furious. Instead, she was clearheaded, her perceptions seeming to be diamond sharp.

When Lisa had tapped away down the hall, Cornelia called for Amanda. "Find the small black leather case with

172

brass clasps. It was packed with my most important papers. I believe we put it into the roll top desk in the study, in the locked drawer."

As she waited for Amanda to return, she blessed Lucius. Though she'd pushed aside his warnings about David, all through the dreamlike time of that relationship; once it was all but over she took his advice. She had done what he asked. Now that was going to be the salvation of her niece, though it was also going to hurt her deeply.

Amanda returned with the black case. She handed it to Cornelia, her expression wry, for she knew what it contained.

In it was the last cruel letter that David had written to her, after she sent him away. She seldom allowed herself, through the years, to think of it, but she had kept it safe.

If he had tried to make problems for her, she would have made it public. Luckily, that had not been necessary.

Beneath the envelope was a plastic box holding a cassette tape. In it was the tape she had recorded of her last interview with David. That had caused her qualms of conscience, but she'd done as Lucius asked and turned on the recorder to her stereo, when he tapped on her door on his way to what she knew would be their last meeting.

She opened the letter and stared down at the lines, which had lost their power to hurt:

Cornelia—

I cannot believe what you have done. I knew from the first that you are a cold and unfeeling woman, but I had not thought you were so cruel.

After the years during which I have been devoted to you, without asking anything in return (except a lot of money, she interjected silently), you have turned me away as if I were an incompetent servant.

In my own defense, I must reply to some of the things you said. Despite your terrible temper, your inconsistent disposition, and your much overrated career, I have loved you.

You seem to worship that career at the expense of any human relationship. I cannot understand that and I never will.

You are not a great dancer. I have seen far better ones. There are infinitely better choreographers.

You have been competent, but you are past your prime, and you will find, when you are alone and shunned by those flocking about your success, that you will wish you still had the devotion of—

David

It was a masterful attempt to make her feel not only guilty but fearful of loneliness in her old age. It had not done that, for she knew that she was doing something unique and important. She knew that she had a handful of friends who would never abandon her.

It must have rankled when she forged ahead from triumph to triumph, creating a unique spot for her work in the annals of dance. That last paragraph was supposed to cut her down to size, and it had not.

She did not need to listen to the tape. Every word was engraved on her mind. That had been a painful time, and she wondered at her folly in allowing it to happen.

It had been a sort of early midlife crisis, she supposed. She had, in her mid-thirties, resigned herself to the fact that she would never have a real private life, no child, no home. David had been a sort of late-blooming substitute for those things.

But that was irrelevant. Lisa was the relevant factor. It was going to be hard to tell her what David was really like, for the girl was as hard-headed as Cornelia had ever been. It was going to be painful.

Amanda brought her cup of broth, which was all she could now manage to swallow. She could see, in her mind, the table, set with colorful pottery.

Eric would be arguing with Amos about cattle and crops. David would be listening, his boredom well concealed, catching Lisa's eye with meaningful glances as often as he could.

She sipped the soup and looked up at those happy young girls, on their way to church on a brilliant Fall morning. Their lives would lie along familiar roads, posted with unequivocal signs all along the way.

Their kin had all walked that road for generations, and tracks would tell them where their parents' feet had passed. Sounds behind them would herald the coming of their own children, in time.

How peaceful it would be to go the worn routes, to do the things others did, without having to break new trails. It would be easy to pursue things that caused no ripples of criticism or of complaint. She longed, for a single heartbeat, to know such a life, such thoughtless happiness.

Such terrible sameness!

She laughed aloud, ignoring the pain in her chest. Many were suited to the well-worn roads. Not she.

She had chosen the only road for her, the only way she could have borne to travel. This was as near as she was capable of coming to the joy those youngsters shared, the way of life that was theirs.

She finished the soup and pushed the tray aside. While she waited for Lisa, she closed her eyes. Rest would be useful, for the interview she was about to have was not going to be easy or painless. She knew herself, and she knew her niece.

What had she done when Lucius tried to tell her about David?

She had gone into a cold fury, denied any possibility of truth in her lawyer's allegations. She had made a fool of herself. Lisa would be no different.

Lisa was also quick of mind. If Lucius had possessed hard evidence for his case, that would have shaken her convictions. He did not have it.

But she had.

Chapter Twenty-Six

A Rocky Road

Cornelia slept briefly after lunch. Amanda held everyone at bay until she woke again, the edge of alertness still with her. The rest, however, had not given her any resurgence of strength.

She took her medication, reassuring Amanda as she set aside her glass. "I can do this, my dear. Don't let it upset you so."

"But that bastard hunted down that poor child as if she were a partridge in the fields. She's a spoiled brat, but she doesn't deserve the kind of misery David Beauchamp is going to give her. And it's all just to get back at you!

"And, of course, to put his hands on your property and the money you worked yourself to death to earn. I could kill him!"

"Well, don't. He isn't worth the prison sentence. Besides, can't you see what a pitiful mess of a human being he has turned out to be?"

"I can see the mess. I cannot see the pitifulness," she grumbled. Cornelia stared up at the ceiling, thinking hard. "I understand now why primitive people think that the dying are seers and prophets," she said.

"I can see things that I never suspected. I understand situations and people, and it boggles my mind to think how they puzzled me when I was in the midst of my life.

"I can see David for what he is." She laughed softly, though it joggled her waterlogged body painfully. "He's no figure of romance, as I thought him at one time. No monster

176

with horns and tail, as you see him. No greedy moneygrubber, as Lucius thinks of him. No, he's something else entirely, although he is just a bit of all of those, too."

"What, for God's sake?" Amanda demanded.

"A very small and inadequate person who happens to have been born into a magnificent body and a good social position. A tiny mind, with all the scope of a squirrel on a treadmill, behind the face of a Greek god. A pitiable excuse for a human being who tries desperately to maintain his disguise as someone to be reckoned with."

She gasped, and Amanda pushed another pillow behind her to elevate her head and shoulders.

"You're talking too much. You are going to have more than enough talking to do, in a bit, so don't waste your breath on me. I don't want to see that son-of-a-bitch as anything but what I know he is."

Cornelia drew a ragged breath. "Call them in, Amanda. I'm not going to get better, and I must do this while I have the strength."

Lisa came alone, for their promised talk. She went pale when she saw Cornelia's face. "Aunt, are you all right?" she whispered.

"My dear child, I'm dying. By inches, of course, but getting very near the end. I am sometimes worse and sometimes better. Today I'm worse, but there are things we must clear up. I don't know if there will be another chance for us to do it." She paused, breathing heavily.

Lisa looked wary. "Things besides the estate?"

"Things like David. Who asked me to marry him, years ago. I had sense enough to say no, even though I thought I was desperately in love with him. And at the last I sent him about his business. Lucius warned me. Amanda warned me. I couldn't see past his charm, his education, his beauty, for too long a time."

"I don't believe this! David told me you'd be against our marrying, but I had no idea you'd go this far! Making up such a ridiculous story!" There was a red spot on each of Lisa's cheeks, and her eyes were dangerously bright.

"I sent him away when it became obvious that he was using my charge accounts irresponsibly, as well as taking

177

money from my apartment. He is a kept man, Lisa. He always will be. If you marry him without telling him about the trust, he will be gone like a shot, once he learns about it. If you tell him now, he will be gone even faster."

Lisa rose, skidding her chair backward. "I will not listen to this!"

"Then listen to this." Cornelia pushed the cassette tape across the counterpane. "There's a player in the stereo in the living room. The others will come in here with me while you play it. Once you hear it, come back and face David. Or if you can't bear to face him, send Amanda. She would love the chance to tell him off. Go now, as a favor to your dying relative. Please!"

Lisa passed her father and David in the hall, just outside the door. David gave her a long glance, as he entered the bedroom and took his place in the chair she had vacated. Eric was quiet and watchful, waiting for whatever was about to happen.

Cornelia smiled. The letter was folded flat and tucked in the plastic case holding the tape. Lisa would get everything through those two items, without another word from anyone. It was all there, and if it didn't convince the girl, nothing would.

Cornelia reached for her brother's hand. "Did you check out the place?" she asked.

"Sure did. We need some new fence along the southwest line. I told Amos I'd send posts and wire tomorrow. He can get someone to help him with the work."

He ran his fingers through his graying hair. "I thought the cattle looked good. Fat and healthy. All the rain after the hurricane helped the grass a lot. It's still jumping." His eyes held a question.

She quirked an eyebrow in their old signal for Wait! They chatted uneasily, killing time until Lisa rejoined them. David kept glancing toward the door, as if he expected her to arrive, but she didn't come.

Half an hour passed without a sign from the girl. Cornelia was certain she was crying in the bathroom. It was what Watson women of the stronger variety did, in private, with nobody at hand to ask questions. Then, being a Watson to the bone, however much she might have been affected by modern attitudes, Lisa would come back and face David.

That would prove some things Cornelia wanted desperately to believe. Lisa seemed superficial—wimpy, she had always called it. But beneath that there must be the tough stock that had pioneered this difficult country. Someplace inside Lisa was the intelligence and problem solving ability that Cornelia's parents had possessed.

When Lisa came, it was with a crisp clacking of heels on the hardwood floor. Something about the staccato rhythm of those steps made David sit up as if he were alarmed.

Eric began to grin, very slowly. Cornelia quirked her brow again and began to relax.

Lisa had never looked so beautiful. Her dark chestnut hair swirled with the vigor of her movement, as she surged into the room. Her eyes snapped with fire, and her color was brilliant.

She went to Cornelia and laid the plastic case on the bed by her hand. "Thank you," she said. "I wouldn't have believed anything else."

David stood and moved toward her. "What has this woman been telling you? I knew she'd try and come between us—she always had her eye on me, in the old days. I had to run for my life!"

"For her checkbook would be more like it," Lisa said. "For her charge cards. For her social connections!" The electricity of her anger filled the room.

"You simply cannot believe that!" he protested.

"Oh, but I can. I read your letter. I heard what you said to her, the last time you visited Cornelia. You—gigolo!

"You found me—how long did that take?—just so you could get your hands on the assets you always wanted."

"You heard...how?"

"She taped you, you idiot! Cornelia's no fool who can be used and manipulated and hornswoggled. She taped you!" The words came out as a crow of triumph.

Cornelia could see the traces of tears on Lisa's cheeks, the telltale red lines in her eyes, but nobody else noticed, she was certain. Lisa had cried out her hurt and grief. Then she had stormed in to tell David off in the best Watson tradition. She was, indeed, of the tough old stock.

David wasn't handling things as well. He turned his face toward Cornelia, hatred in his eyes. "You...old...bitch!" he said, his voice thick and ugly.

Eric rose leisurely from the rocker. He put his hand on David's shoulder, turned him slightly to face him, and hit him, deliberately and forcefully, on the point of the chin. David went down with a thud.

"Amos!" Eric stepped over his victim and went to the door. "Amos! Come help me drag this carrion out of the house. And tell Ella to call a cab from town. We don't want him here." He turned to his sister. "I'll call Cyn and tell her to have his things waiting outside the house. I don't want the stink of him to penetrate the walls."

Lisa dropped to the edge of the bed. Cornelia reached to pull her head onto her own shoulder. The tears, so bravely suppressed, came again, dampening the eyelet frill of her nightgown.

Amos, imperturbable as always, arrived and lifted one side of the man as Eric took the other. They hustled him away down the corridor. Cornelia thought she heard his toes dragging along behind them.

Then the room disappeared in a swirl of mist. The pressure of Lisa's head on her shoulder thinned to nothing. Cornelia felt herself pulled away, drowning in a sea of fluid and pain.

Again, she stood beside the stone bell in the clearing. The hammer was in her hand.

"Now?" she asked.

"No," came the strong young version of her own voice. "Not yet, and not here. You have not endured to the end, and you have not found your own place. Be patient. You have accomplished one thing. There are more. There are always more. Wait, and endure."

The bell was gone; the clearing vanished. She was someplace she had always known. Darkness surrounded her. Sparks of light came into being. Stars...she was again in the spaces she had dreamed as a child, staring at suns as an equal, from their own perspectives.

She lost contact with her body, though she felt, still, some tie to it. All of her that mattered was wandering among the stars, marveling at the complexity of the motions, the colors, the varieties of worlds and systems she could see, passing through them like a mist.

There came a pricking at her arm.

Jonathan, ready as always to recall her to her duty!

She sighed and opened her eyes. "Do you truly have to do that?" she asked.

"It doesn't keep you alive. It just helps you to breathe. Come now, don't you prefer to breathe painlessly?"

"I suppose so. We had a real set-to here, today. Did Amanda tell you?" she asked.

"She did, indeed. It sounds like a job well done." He leaned back in the rocker and lit his pipe. "You continue to amaze me, Cornelia."

"I seem to amaze myself, from time to time. You know, Jonathan, dying is truly interesting. It's true—you can understand things you never knew existed. I'm finding that out more and more." She felt the room spin gently about her, but that didn't worry her, now.

"Amanda told me all about what happened. Did you ever suspect you would have any use for that tape you made?" he asked.

She slowed her spinning and smiled. "I didn't really suspect. But I had a feeling that it might come in handy, one day. And it did! Lisa is as hard-headed as I am. Nothing else would have worked."

Jonathan rose and looked down. "I can see that you're a bit disoriented, but I wanted to tell you something. I brought you a present."

"Jonathan! You know there's nothing I need. I have more than I can think about, now."

"This is something you will like. Amanda unwrapped it, and I'm going to hold it up for you to see. Here! Look!"

He reached down for something leaning against the foot of the bed and hitched it upward with some effort.

She gasped with pleasure and wonder.

It was a large canvas. Worlds and suns and moons were painted against a midnight background. They were connected by web-fine silvery lines that bound them together in intricate loops. Orbits, gravitational fields, all their patterns of interconnections were woven about them.

She sighed with satisfaction. It was the place of her vision. "What is it called?" she asked faintly.

"*Upon a Road of Stars*," he said, his tone gentle. "Do you want me to hang it now?"

"No," she said. "Not yet. It will be the last. The very last. I will go out into it and never come back again."

CHAPTER TWENTY-SEVEN

UP ST. SWITHIN'S LANE

It was three days before Cornelia was alert enough to notice anything. When she came to herself, Eric was in the rocking chair beside the bed, his head cocked awkwardly against its back, his mouth open to emit burbling snores. She knew she must have gone very near to the edge, this time.

She lay quietly, looking about the room in which she had been born. Each time she awoke, now, she did that, imprinting the familiar walls and furniture into her memory. So much of her past and that of her family was contained here... she faintly regretted leaving it behind.

There was another painting on the wall at the foot of her bed, for Amanda still changed it every day, giving her something fresh to study. This was not one of her favorites...she had worked her way through most of those. This was a rather pale watercolor of a street in an English village.

A duck pond on the right balanced a row of cottages on the left. The lane hooked off beyond the last of the cottages.

She had explored so many paintings in the past month that it was no effort of the imagination to follow the roads in them. She found herself beside the duck pond at once, listening to the quarrelsome quacks, the erratic splashings of the fowl.

Someone across the way was singing a lullaby— probably for a baby's nap, as it was still early afternoon.

The warm mellowness of English sunlight gilded the planes of the stone walls that edged the minute gardens. It trimmed the hollyhocks and the stocks with brightness and turned the pale stone to a glorious shade of glowing amber. It also lit the crooked sign at the bend of the road.

"St. Swithin's Lane," the Gothic script announced. She chuckled and made the turn into the sort of dark street she had thought belonged only in a city.

Narrow brick shop fronts shouldered each other along the way, thrusting faded signs into the notice of the passerby. Second stories extended over the road, shutting away the brilliance of the sky.

She noted the signs, in passing:

GREENGROCER

HATCHETT-HAMMERSLEY, BUTCHER

FINE TAILORING, MAUDESLEY AND SONS

One in particular took her fancy. It said, simply,

NOTIONS

She knew just what it would mean in her own country, but she wondered what it might portend here in a village. Small gifts and useful items? Possibly, but she had a feeling it was not that simple.

She opened the door, hearing a bell tinkle lightly above her head. The shop was so narrow that she could have touched her fingertips to each side wall, if she flung her arms wide. It seemed to be empty, at first, as she peered through the gloom to see what it might contain.

There was a glass-fronted case running down the wall to her right. It had four shelves, counting the top, and on them were items so dim and dusty that it was hard to make out what they might be. As she bent and put her nose near the glass, trying to see, there came a quiet step at the rear of the shop.

"And have you a notion for me today?"

She straightened to look at the woman who now was swimming toward her through the murky light. As if realizing how dark the place was, the woman reached to turn on a lamp in a stained-glass shade. It shed multicolored light over the case and the woman herself.

She was a strange looking person. Dark-haired, her olive face so pale that she almost seemed ill, she was tall and slender, dressed in an alpaca gown that would have seemed a bit dated during the reign of Victoria. But her eyes were brilliant and her expression intelligent.

"I'm sorry," said Cornelia. "I really have no idea what you might sell here. I was intrigued by your sign. In my country, notions seem to mean something different."

"Ah, an American. Yes, indeed, they are different here. I do not sell notions. I accept them and put them away."

This time, I am certainly dreaming, thought Cornelia, though she didn't allow a word to pass her lips. She smiled instead. "Do explain," she said to the woman. "I am very interested."

"Then come into my parlor at the rear of the shop. Have a cup of tea, and I shall explain my business to you. Perhaps you have some choice item for me and do not realize it."

Her parlor was snug—small, of course, but adequate for the pair of them. Cornelia sat on a worn velvet chair and sipped Lapsang-Oolong from a Belleek cup so fragile that she hesitated to touch her lips too firmly to its rim.

"I deal in misconceptions. Notions, in the common parlance," said the woman. "I am, by the bye, Madame Lessiter.

"My family have been in the trade for generations, and my late husband entered it when we married and worked with me for as long as he lived. I have his notions set aside in a special cupboard. A sentimental conceit, you might call it, but I allow myself that one weakness."

"And the shelves out there? Are the things in them all the misconceptions you have acquired? Do you buy them? Trade for them?" Cornelia felt disoriented, a bit dizzy.

"I accept them as a favor to those who are happy to be rid of them. They are not salable—indeed, who would deliberately take up something that another has acknowledged to be nothing but folly?"

Cornelia took another sip to cover her confusion. As dreams went, this one was highly unusual. "And how do you find your customers? How do you know that they have something to give you?" she asked.

"They find me," replied Madame Lessiter. She stirred her tea reflectively. "It seems there is something about my shop that attracts only those who need my services.

"Nobody else ever enters. If someone does come, as you have done, then I know he must have a notion needing to be discarded onto my shelves."

"I am here," said Cornelia, her tone doubtful, "but I thought I had already discarded all my misconceptions, over the months of my illness. I have been shedding them steadily."

Madame Lessiter stood and beckoned her toward the front of the shop. "Come and see my stock. It might remind you of whatever it is you need to let go."

She lit more lamps as they moved up the narrow space beside the case. Spheres of glassy substance glimmered on the shelves, each containing a different sort of swirl of colors and shapes.

"Here," the woman said, slipping aside a front panel and lifting out a sphere. "This is the notion of a famous beauty.

"She thought, like Snow White's stepmother, that she was the most beautiful woman ever to live. She went on to become a useful and loving person, once she rid herself of this notion."

Cornelia squinted into the glassy depths. "Faces!" she said, turning it about. "Like masks, all lovely and tiny and far away."

The woman took the sphere and set it on the shelf. "Look at this," she said, bringing out another. "It will tell you something of the world in which we live."

This was a dark-shaded ball, inside of which a tumble of purple and green and black chased itself about like a trio of serpents, trying to swallow one another.

"He is a politician. He meant well, in the beginning, but he fell prey, as so many do, to expedience and self-indulgence. He came to our village as he campaigned for office, and his wife dragged him into my shop. Literally dragged him, protesting and dragging his heels."

Madame Lessiter smiled grimly. "We wrung this from him, the pair of us, and not without a lot of protest and outcry. When it was all contained in its ball, the poor man stood up and stared at it. 'That was inside me?' he asked us."

Cornelia felt herself beginning to giggle. "If I had to guess what was inside a politician, I probably would guess purple-green goop," she said.

"He was a changed man," Madame continued. "His wife gave up her action for divorce. His children began staying about him, instead of running away when he came home.

"Of course, he lost the election. But he went into one of the Ministries, and now he is doing vital and valuable work for his country. Honestly and honorably."

Cornelia stopped in her tracks. "Ego," she said. "That's the common denominator, here. Ego. The belief that you and your affairs are at the top of the heap, more important than anything else.

"And I, too, have a misconception in that area. I will bet my boots on it."

Madame nodded approvingly. "I can do a reading to find the problem, but it is usually better for the person to locate it herself. It extracts so much more neatly, and there seldom is a problem of regrowth. What have you decided to give me?"

"My gut feeling that I'm the greatest thing ever to happen to the field of ballet. My smug acceptance of the 'fact' that my original works are the very best ever. That is what I will give you to add to your collection. And I'll pay you a bonus, too."

"That is how we live and prosper," Madame Lessiter said, smiling. "People are usually most grateful to rid themselves of destructive errors.

"Come back to the parlor. We shall busy ourselves with removing your notion."

They returned to the parlor. Madame poured more tea, and they nibbled a seedcake. Then she indicated that Cornelia should recline on the horsehair sofa. "Think of all the things you have been proudest of doing," said the woman. She held the glass sphere close to Cornelia's face. "Project it all into the ball."

Cornelia thought of *The Life of the Heart.* Of her own favorite performances. Of the press clippings and the rave reviews and the hangers-on who assured her that she was the greatest dancer of all time, ignoring the greats like Karsavina and Elssler and Pavlova.

What nonsense! She had controlled her body competently. She had put her heart into her work. People had responded to the things she pulled from the depths of her mind and her spirit. That was all.

The glass clouded. She had seen, before, only her own reflection in the curved shape. Now it began to fill with something pale, wispy, full of motion. She watched with amazement as tiny dancers took shape inside, moving about as if gravity had never been invented, dancing on the inner surface of the sphere.

She saw herself, a minikin figure, leaping, whirling, spinning on one toe, sinking into a reverence. She laughed.

She had been good...a bit better than good, actually, she realized. But it had nothing to do with what she now was or what she was about to become. All of that was irrelevant, pushed away into the past.

She rose and went with Madame into the shop. The woman placed the cloudy sphere on a shelf near the front of the place.

"We are becoming crowded," Madame Lessiter said. "By the time I am gone, my daughter will be hard put to find space for our stock."

Cornelia surveyed the small spot left empty near the door. "You may have to put some into storage," she said. "But do stay in business.

"I wonder if you could open a branch in the United States? You are sorely needed there."

She began to laugh...and the laughter, shaking her sick body, woke her. For a moment, she could still see the dim shop, the dusty spheres on the glass shelving, the pale face of Madame Lessiter.

Eric sat up with a snort. "You're awake again," he said. "But what's so funny?"

"A dream. Just a dream," said Cornelia. "I went up St. Swithin's lane, around that corner in the painting up there. And what a truly strange journey that was!"

"You've been out for so long that we had to feed you in- travenously. Jonathan sent a nurse to stay. She's off duty, right now, but she'll be here in a bit. Why don't you eat something and surprise her?"

Cornelia shook her head. "No. I have lost any appetite I had. I have lost any need to keep this thing alive. Lisa is safe. I've made friends with my kin. What in the world am I wait- ing around for?"

She took his hand. "I truly am ready to go, Bro."

Eric's eyes crinkled at the corners. His mouth twisted painfully. "I know. I know. I would too, if I were in your shoes. But it's hard, Neely. It's really hard!"

"Will you call Lucius?" she asked. "After?"

His fingers tightened on hers. "Yes. I'd intended to, all along. Don't worry, Neely. I'll tend to everything."

She sighed and relaxed. Then she said, "Tell Cynthia to come to see me, will you? We haven't been friends, she and I. I don't want to leave anything undone. Tell her to come out tomorrow. I can't say surely that I'll be here much past that."

Eric touched her cheek very softly with the tip of a fin- ger. "Will do. I'd like that. I hope...but we'll just have to see, won't we?"

Cornelia smiled, but she had no strength to answer.

Chapter Twenty-Eight

Tidying Up

Cynthia arrived at noon the next day. She looked nervous and a bit flustered. Eric saw her into Cornelia's room, kissed his sister on the cheek, and left the two alone. Cornelia knew he had gone to help Amos with the fence-building, champing at the bit until he could get his hands dirty with work.

Cynthia, perched on the rocker like a wren on a twig, stared at her sister-in-law. There was shock in her eyes, for she had not seen Cornelia since she arrived, months before.

"Don't let it bother you," Cornelia said. "My outside has seen better days, but inside I am the same tough, nonconformist person you always felt so nervous about. What happened to us, I wonder?

"Was it Coral's nattering? Was it Emily's suspicions?" She sighed. "I would truly have liked to be better friends with my brother's wife, for I love him devotedly."

Cynthia twisted her soft hands in her lap. She looked very cool and smart in her cream-colored pantsuit, as well as terribly uncomfortable in this room where her husband had been born.

"No," she said. "It wasn't what they said, though they did go on a lot. It was Eric. I was jealous, I think."

"Of me? I'm his sister! Why?"

"Because you were always there, in his mind. I could feel him thinking about you, no matter how long it had been since he'd seen you. I knew the two of you could somehow think together, read each other's minds, it seemed at times.

"I never was able to manage to do that. I would have given anything to be inside Eric's thoughts, the way you've always been."

"I am going to be gone, very soon," Cornelia said. "Eric is going to need you more than ever before, for he is going to miss me a great deal.

"You are right—we have had an especially close and affectionate relationship. We have been better friends than siblings often manage to become."

Cynthia looked down at her hands. "I know that. I just wonder if I'll be enough for him, once you are gone. I haven't done a brilliant job of being a wife, Cornelia. I'm not super-bright, like Eric. I'm not talented, like you. I know it, and I've tried to find things I can do, but nothing seems to work for me."

Cornelia would have felt pity, but she pushed the emotion back firmly. Pity was seldom useful, and at this point it would be an obstacle to her purpose.

"You have made Eric love you for twenty-two years," she said. "Even through the rough spots, he has never wavered. You had Lisa, who has been the joy of his life and who is going to be a winner, once she gets all the way over Fool's Hill. We all have to climb that, at one time or another, and she's just about made it. She came through like a thoroughbred yesterday. Did Eric tell you?"

Cynthia blushed. "I should have seen through that man. But you were the one...."

"Good Lord, Cynthia! I was the first one in the family he hornswoggled! It was experience, not good sense, that made me warn Lisa.

"David can charm the birds out of the trees, when he tries, and he was trying his best, believe me. It was worth his while to fool you all, while he got his hooks into Lisa's inheritance."

Cynthia relaxed. Her hands unclenched. Her color returned to normal.

"I'm sorry we were never close, Cornelia. I never knew you could be so...so friendly."

"We were like a couple of tomcats under a tin tub," Cornelia chuckled. "You bowed up at me. I bowed right back at you. Stupid, isn't it, for two sensible adults to behave that way?

"Even when we were kids, we were apt to steer clear of each other, but now I want us to part as friends. It will mean a lot to Eric, as well as to me." She held out her hand.

The effort was too much. The extended hand dropped onto the counterpane.

Cynthia caught it in both of hers. She held it quietly, as Cornelia wheezed for breath.

Something passed between the two. Concern for the man they both loved, perhaps. Belated respect.

Cornelia felt that she was a relay runner, passing the wand to the next in line. Cynthia would do. She never would have guessed it before, but she would definitely do.

She struggled to breathe. Something was smothering her, and she pulled her hand from Cynthia's grasp and caught at her throat.

She was lifted into a sitting position by a pair of arms that were stronger than she could have guessed. "Here, let me prop you up. Do you have medicine for that?"

"Table. Box."

With easy efficiency, Cynthia got the tablet down her, with water to wash it along. Then she perched on the edge of the bed, watching Cornelia anxiously.

The drug relaxed her, easing her struggling lungs. She settled against the pillows with a sigh. "Take care of them, Cynthia. I'm depending on you."

The woman stood straight as a soldier accepting a commission. "I will, Cornelia. God be with you."

She turned blindly and left the room.

Amanda entered. She must have waited in the hall. "You all right?"

"No. But it's the time for that. Call Eric, dear. I want to talk to him."

"You're wearing yourself out, you know."

"It's now or never. Call Eric, dear, please."

She could hear Amanda's unvoiced protest as she stumped away down the hall toward the kitchen. In a short while, Eric came in to sit in the rocker his wife had just left.

"Anything I can do?"

"I must tidy up the loose ends, Bro. Read me the will and the codicil. Right there in the drawer of the bedside table. I want to be certain everything is just right."

He took the thick sheaf of legal-sized papers and began reading, his voice low and steady, though she heard the effort he made to keep it that way.

The bequests were in order. The addendum regarding the foundation to oversee the over-aged dancers was flawless. Lisa's inheritance, with the attached safeguards, was sound. The farm and the livestock all went to her, under Eric's supervision. The household goods, which had belonged to the family for three generations, were to be divided as Coral, Eric, and Cynthia decided among them.

"Add a line. I'll sign it, and it should go through all right. We'll get Amanda to witness it," she said.

He got a pen and held it ready. "Shoot," he said. "I'll write."

"Mom's books and stories are to be on permanent loan to Special Collections at the University. Okay?"

He grinned. "Just right. I'll see to it myself, and I should have thought of that. We can't risk having them lost or destroyed." He scribbled busily and then read back the lines he had written.

"Just right. Thank you, Eric."

"Anything else?"

"Send in Amos and Ella. I want to speak to them."

They came in shyly, though not a day passed that one or the other didn't come into the sickroom to help her with something. Amos sat in the recliner, Ella in the rocking chair. They looked as if they had been crying.

"You have been my friends," Cornelia said, her voice only a husky whisper. "I want you to know I have made a provision in my will. You are to be the caretakers of the farm and the house for as long as you want to and are able.

"There is an annuity that will take care of you when you decide to retire. And I put it into my will that you may both be buried in the Watson graveyard. I hope that pleases you."

Ella touched her handkerchief to her eyes, but her sob didn't escape. Amos shifted in his chair and swallowed hard. "We're mightily obliged, Ma'am. It's been nice. We've enjoyed doing for you since you came, and we want you to know that we admire you a lot.

"We've been with people, before, who were dying. We've never seen one as easy to get on with or who seems to be doing as much as you have. We've watched you, and neither one of us is as scared of dying as we used to be."

Ella touched her hand. "Thank you, Miss Watson. We're obliged, and we are going to miss you a lot."

Cornelia closed her eyes. She felt too weary to attempt breathing, now. She heard their steps go away quietly and Amanda's come back into the room.

"Eric," she breathed. "Cynthia. Lisa. Please?"

They arrived almost before she had finished and stood at the foot of the Monster Bed.

"Go home now, my dears. With my love. All of you. This is something I must do alone. Nobody can help. Don't grieve, for we've learned a lot, haven't we? All four of us...."

Eric's lips clenched hard. Then he shivered and said, "We have, indeed. Goodbye, Neely. God bless." He shepherded his womenfolk out of the room.

She drifted away for a time. When she returned to her gross body, Jonathan was standing beside her.

"Don't think you can get away without saying goodbye, Cornelia Watson. I have come to think of myself as part of your family, like it or not."

She found that she could still form a smile. "Glad... you're here," she gasped. "Do sit down and...have a cup of tea."

The doctor exploded with laughter.

"My God, Cornelia, who else could crack jokes in the middle of...of...."

"Dying," she finished for him.

"Of dying. You know you're not the only one who has learned a lot. Not a soul lucky enough to be with you, these past months, hasn't had a lot of new things to think about. A sort of post-graduate degree in living."

His face drifted into and out of focus, but she made the effort to speak. "In what? Lord knows, all I've been expert at doing is moving to music."

194

"Determination. Courage—I know, I know! You don't call it that. But it is, you know.

"You've bull-headed your way right through the middle of the most frightening thing that happens to us as human beings, and here you are at the natural end. And you're not afraid, are you?"

She could suddenly see him clearly, along with the rest of the room, the rocker, the ash tree beyond the window. "Not all can do it this way. Or should."

"Probably," he agreed. "But more might try. If one in a hundred could manage what you have done, what a wonderful thing it would be for them!"

But abstractions had withdrawn into the mists that gathered again around the edges of the room. The walls were retreating into vast distances.

The head of the Monster Bed seemed to be growing transparent, and the gargoyle looked startled.

Amanda took her hand. Something wet—tears, of course—fell onto her fingers. She tried to squeeze the calloused palm holding hers.

"Jonathan."

He bent over her. "What, my dear?"

"The painting. *The Road of Stars*. Now...hang it. Please?"

He straightened and left the room. In a moment, his crisp footsteps returned down the hall.

The canvas was in his hands, and he had Amanda take down the painting on the wall. He replaced it with the dark spaces captured in oils in the picture he had given her.

She sighed with pleasure. The weight of the fluid in her body was easing. The pressure on her lungs and the pain in her kidneys was lessening.

She opened her lips to thank him, but there were no words left in her. Dark mist swirled from the corners of the room, touching her with cool tendrils, erasing the familiar furniture, the room, the well-loved faces.

There was a distant rustle. What?

Wind in the ash tree. A farewell whisper from that old friend.

She could still see the painting, which was growing clearer and clearer as she stared at it.

The spaces seemed to lap about her feet. The suns burned with gold and silver fires, and the worlds there reflected them in their spheres of dark green and blue and umber.

She could almost feel those webs of gravity against her skin. It was like walking on a dewy morning through cobwebs hung between the trees, she thought.

She moved forward still more....

CHAPTER TWENTY-NINE

UPON A ROAD OF STARS

The room was gone. The swollen body was all but forgotten as if it had never existed. She moved farther into the spaces, between the suns, among the planets that swung deliberately along their invisible tracks.

Moons were flecks of silver dust. Stars were great presences, outside the system where she walked but still accessible. Waiting for her to find them.

The last link snapped. Her edema-ridden flesh was lost in the darkness behind her.

Cornelia moved, free and fresh and joyful, onto the waiting roads....

A Road of Stars, by Ardath Mayhar

There were always stars;
come fogs or tempests,
they were there
behind the blinded sky.
Within the darkness of her skull
she saw their implacable constancy.

They were always there,
a dazzle of splendor
burning above the paths,
blazing behind closed eyelids.

Across black magnitudes,
she walks upon a road of stars.

ABOUT THE AUTHOR

The author of sixty-two books, more than forty of them published commercially, **ARDATH MAYHAR** began her career in the early eighties with science fiction novels from Doubleday and TSR. Atheneum published several of her young adult and children's novels. Changing focus, she wrote westerns (as **Frank Cannon**) and mountain man novels (as **John Killdeer**). Four prehistoric Indian books under her own name came out from Berkley. Historical western *High Mountain Winter* was published by Berkley Books under the byline **Frances Hurst**.

Recently she has been working with on-line publishers. *A Road of Stars* was her first original novel to appear in print-on-demand format. Many of her out-of-print titles are now available from e-publishers fictionwise.com and renebooks.com; other novels are being reprinted via the Borgo Press Imprint of Wildside Press and Amazon.com.

Now in her seventies, Mayhar was widowed in 1999, after forty-one years of marriage, and has four grown sons. She now works at home, writing short fiction and nonfiction, and doing book doctoring professionally. Her web pages can be found at:

w2.netdot.com/ardathm/ and http://ofearna.us/books/mayhar.html